'Why did you use a false name?'

Leeton's eyes hadn't moved from Ellie's face.

'Did you think I wouldn't find out? Even if I hadn't bothered to research your background, I would have known the moment you got off the boat.'

'I didn't try to deceive you,' she said defensively. 'My boss used my real name when he told you I was coming.'

'And you change names whenever you change jobs?'

'No. Whenever I change husbands,' she said bitterly.

Dear Reader

Marion Lennox gives us a quite spectacular setting in THE LAST EDEN, and two fascinating people in Ellie and Leeton for you to enjoy. In HANDFUL OF DREAMS, Lucy is shocked to inherit a school, and in A BORDER PRACTICE Dr Lyall Balfour is a mystery for physiotherapist Lindy to solve. Dr Rose Gillis has the uncomfortable job of bossing a man who is senior to her in rank in A SONG FOR DR ROSE — Margaret Holt has created a super character in Leigh. Four very different stories, but all enthralling! See you next month.

The Editor

Marion Lennox has had a variety of careers — medical receptionist, computer programmer and teacher. Married, with two young children, she now lives in rural Victoria, Australia. Her wish for an occupation which would allow her to remain at home with her children, her dog and the budgie led her to attempt writing a novel.

Recent titles by the same author:

THE HEALING HEART
WINGS OF HEALING

THE LAST EDEN

BY

MARION LENNOX

To Molly
with Best Wishes
Marion Lennox
x x x

MILLS & BOON LIMITED
ETON HOUSE   18–24 PARADISE ROAD
RICHMOND   SURREY   TW9 1SR

With thanks to Ron whose time in the Antarctic made this book possible, to Pam for her invaluable assistance, to the Public Relations Department of the Australian Antarctic Division, and to the numerous people without whose specialised knowledge and generosity in sharing it this book could not have been written.

First published in Great Britain 1993
by Mills & Boon Limited

© Marion Lennox 1993

Australian copyright 1993
Philippine copyright 1993
This edition 1993

ISBN 0 263 78137 2

Set in 10 on 11 pt Linotron Baskerville
03-9306-58147

Typeset in Great Britain by Centracet, Cambridge
Made and printed in Great Britain

CHAPTER ONE

'So that's it, Dr Michaels. The boat leaves for Antarctica in two weeks, and I want you on it.'

In the twenty-seven years since Dr Eleanor Michaels had uttered her first sentence, she had been shocked into silence three times.

The first had been at nursery school when Sammy Coad had lost control and declared the source of the puddle was his best friend, Ellie. The second was twenty-two years later when the same Samuel Coad, brilliant up-and-coming barrister, had conceded that he was indeed having an affair and he wished to divorce Ellie. The third was now.

Ellie sank into a spare armchair in her boss's office and let her jaw drop. She stared at the middle-aged man in front of her, searching for some trace of humour on his broad face. There was none. Walter Mitchen was not known for jokes.

Walter was reaching for the phone as he watched her. Despite his serious expression he was amused at Ellie's reaction. In the time he had employed Dr Michaels he had never known her at a loss for words, and he wondered how long she would take to get her breath back.

He liked Dr Ellie Michaels. Her background was perfect for her career as a medical journalist. She was a competent doctor with a flair for writing which made even the most difficult medical concepts easy for the general public to understand. In the two years since she had joined the staff of *Our Planet's Health* she had pulled in some of the best articles the magazine had printed.

She was slightly built, vivacious and friendly. With

her soft brown hair cut in an elfin haircut, big brown eyes and freckles, she was a picture of innocence, and in the jeans and big bright sweaters she favoured she looked about fourteen.

During interviews her image worked like a charm. Often the high-powered magnates behind international drug companies, or civic officials intent on whitewashing important health issues, were stunned when *Our Planet's Health* hit the streets to learn just how much they had revealed to this slip of a girl. Her medical training and sheer intelligence made her one of the most competent medical reporters in the country, and Walter was still blessing his good fortune for her decision to leave the *Daily* to join his staff.

She didn't look competent or efficient now. Ellie just looked stunned.

'I'll call in Jo,' Walter said affably to the open-mouthed girl in front of him. 'She can do the legwork in organising flights and visas. Some of the things we've bought are going to have to be changed too. I think Frank's long johns might be a trifle too large.' For the first time Walter permitted himself a smile.

Dr Michaels shook her head, as if trying to escape a bad dream. She took a deep breath, fighting for words. Finally she leaned forward, grabbed the receiver from her boss's hand and slammed it down on to the cradle.

'Let's just leave your secretary out of this for the moment.' Her voice was a squeak.

Walter raised his eyebrows. 'Is something wrong, Ellie?'

'Is something wrong?' Ellie gaped at him. 'You tell me to pack my bags because I'm going to the Antarctic to interview Leeton Connor, and you ask is something wrong?' She fought to get her voice back on an even keel. 'Walter, if you weren't my boss, I'd say you had rocks in your head.'

He smiled. 'It's never stopped you in the past, Ellie.'

Despite her shock, Ellie was forced into a glimmer of a smile, and Walter relaxed. He knew he would have his way.

'Ellie, there's no one else,' he explained. 'Connor's said he'll have one representative from our magazine on site, and he doesn't want someone who's never heard of thermogenesis, or doesn't understand the operation of BIOMASS.'

'Thermogenesis. . .the ability of the body to produce heat,' Ellie said slowly. She gave a rueful grin. 'Myself, I prefer to rely on a hot-water bottle.'

Walter ignored her flippancy. 'And BIOMASS. . .the Biological Investigation of Marine Antarctic Systems and Stocks? You've done articles with Frank before on the aims of the organisation.'

'Yes.' Ellie's tone was cautious.

'Then you know it's an international group with the aim of understanding the Antarctic marine ecosystem. Connor's one of the principals behind the organisation.'

'Leeton Connor!' Ellie shook her head in disbelief. 'I didn't know that.' She frowned. 'Why isn't it public knowledge?'

'For some reason he's elected to work quietly behind the scenes.' Walter looked across at her. 'Does that change your views on the man?'

She frowned. 'I am surprised,' she admitted. 'I didn't know Leeton Connor could be involved in anything so worthwhile.'

'It's true, though,' Walter said firmly. 'He's working in closely with C.C.A.M.L.R. — the Convention and Conservation of Marine Living Resources — and also the UN Food and Agricultural Organisation. Both those organisations you know well, and Leeton won't have to spend half his time answering stupid questions. You understand medical terminology already, and any specific concepts relating to vet science I know you'll pick up fast.'

Ellie shook her head. 'I'm a doctor,' she said. 'And Leeton Connor is a veterinarian. Why not send Frank?' Frank was senior to Ellie on the magazine's reporting team, and a qualified vet.

'Frank's wife is having a baby.'

She looked at Walter appraisingly. 'Let me get this straight,' she said at last. 'The plan is for me to fly to Tasmania, go south on one of the ice-breakers used to supply the Antarctic bases, interview Leeton Connor and come home again.'

'That's right.'

'The whole trip should take, what, about six weeks?'

'Yes——'

'Then why can't Frank go?' Ellie broke in. 'Frank's wife has only just learned she's pregnant. He'd even be home in time for antenatal classes.'

Walter looked up at her and then down at the pad in front of him. With his gold fountain-pen he was doodling in spirals down a sheet of copy.

'Ellie, it's the end of the Antarctic summer,' he said finally. 'You'll be going down with the last supply ship for the season. There's a risk.'

'A risk?'

'Of the ship being locked into the ice. It's happened before. You stay stuck in the ice until the beginning of the next season.' He met her gaze honestly. 'It's unlikely, but, as I said, it's happened in the past. Frank says he won't take that risk, and in the circumstances I can't force him.'

'But you'll force me.' Ellie sank back into her chair, her face still.

Walter laid down his pen, rose and went to the window. His twelfth-floor office looked out over the grey and sleet-filled streets of Manhattan. Without looking back he started to speak.

'Ellie, this story is important. Whatever Dr Leeton Connor does is news, big news. If we ran an article on what colour socks he preferred we'd increase our circulation. Instead of changing his socks, though, he's immersed himself in vet research with the aim of preservation of Antarctica's wildlife. It's a story that this magazine can't afford to ignore.' He hesitated. 'And you're the only person in the position to get it for us.'

Ellie nodded silently. *Our Planet's Health* was a fledgling magazine devoted to health issues of international importance. Its circulation was small, but growing. Featuring a story on Leeton Connor, she had to admit, would give the magazine the sort of push that Walter craved. She sighed and closed her eyes.

'Walter, I can't,' she said bleakly. 'I see your reasons, but. . .' She stopped, then burst out impatiently, 'Walter, you know the last article I wrote on Dr Connor.'

'When you were working for the *Daily*?' Amusement was back in Walter's voice. 'I think we've all heard about it. It was certainly sensational.'

Sensational. It had definitely been that.

Ellie thought back to the last time she had seen Leeton Connor. The public were not admitted to the staff offices of the *Daily*, but then Dr Leeton Connor was not 'the public'. With his immaculate grooming, his staggering good looks and his aura of absolute power and wealth, he had simply walked past the security men as if they didn't exist, to front her in her office.

'He called me a muck-raking, filthy-minded little bitch,' Ellie said desperately. 'He said he would do anything in his power to see I lost my job. If I hadn't quit of my own accord I'm sure he would have managed it.'

Walter shook his head. 'That was two years ago, Ellie,' he said firmly. 'And this is too important an assignment for a two-year-old altercation to be taken into consideration. He's agreed to a representative from this magazine. That's you.'

'He's agreed to Frank.'

'I've already contacted the base camp to let them know Frank won't be coming. Connor got back to me last night. I told him you would be on the ship instead.'

'Me?' she queried.

'You. And in fact he was pleased we were providing him with a doctor instead of a vet. It seems he's worried about one of his men, so I assured him you'd bring full medical supplies. The only problem for him was that you were female. He says it's likely to cause complications.'

'I can imagine,' Ellie said drily. The image of Leeton Connor's 'stable' of women flitted through her mind.

Walter shook his head. 'Not in the way you mean, Ellie. The man has practical things to consider, such as sleeping arrangements. I soon told him you wouldn't expect any undue consideration; that you were sensible and used to rough conditions.'

Ellie grimaced. 'Rough conditions, maybe,' she agreed. 'But Antarctica?' She eyed Walter shrewdly. 'Did he agree?'

'Yes.'

'Why?'

'As I said, he can use you as a doctor,' Walter said bluntly. 'And he needs the publicity we can give him almost as much as we need the publicity he can give us. He's been in the Antarctic for over twelve months, co-ordinating a small group of world-acclaimed veterinarians in a study of man's impact on the wildlife of the region. Now he's about to leave. He's written excellent scientific papers, which frankly, to the layman, are incomprehensible. What he wants is something written for everyone to understand, and he knows as well as we do that he'll get much more satisfactory coverage from an on-site reporter. If the articles are good we'll pass them on to the mass media, after we've printed them first, of course. It could have the results Connor is looking for.'

'So he has to have me,' Ellie said slowly. Then she met Walter's eyes and said directly, 'Walter, did you spell out clearly who I am?'

'I did,' he said innocently 'E.L.L.I.E.M.I.C.H.A.E.L.S. He wrote it down.'

Ellie sighed. 'You mean you didn't tell him.'

Walter sighed wryly. 'That you and the Dr Eleanor Coad who wrote for the *Daily* are one and the same person? Do you think I'm crazy? Connor might be pushed for publicity, but there are limits.'

Ellie stood up and regarded her boss with anger. 'So how do you think he'll feel when I turn up?'

'Maybe in an anorak, with snow on your face, he won't recognise you,' Walter said innocently.

She shook her head impatiently. 'Walter, that's nuts and you know it. All you'll be doing is wasting the magazine's money sending me down there.'

'No.' Walter met her look with the expression of one who had considered, judged and accurately assessed the risks. 'I won't. Connor needs this publicity and he won't let personal animosity get in the way of promoting his cause. Sure he'll be angry, but by the time you're there it'll be too late to insist on someone else coming down. He either gives the story to you, forgets the idea or waits another year down there. There's only one choice.'

'But. . .' Ellie's voice had risen again '. . .have you considered my position? It's intolerable.'

'Ellie, I want that story,' Walter said quietly. 'If I say you can't go, then Connor will approach another magazine. There's none that could cover it the way we could, and you know it. With your combination of medical skills, photographic ability and writing, you are *the* person for the job.' He put his hands together on the desk and regarded her seriously. 'Ellie, I'm asking you to put your personal feelings aside. Get your priorities right.'

She glared at him, baffled. She knew she should hand in her resignation on the spot rather than do this crazy thing. And yet. . .

Since her marriage had ended, Ellie's life had changed direction. The clothes, the money, the social life that had been part of her life with Sam had ceased to be important. Maybe they had never been important to her. But they had been important to Sam. . . As her medicine wasn't.

By the time she had finished medical school, Ellie's career was straining her marriage to breaking-point.

She and Sam had considered themselves a pair since childhood. She had never thought of marriage to anyone else, and they had married soon after high school. Sure, Ellie was a medical student and Sam was in law school, but they were proud of each other and in love. Why wait?

As Sam's legal career had demanded more of his time, however, he'd changed. Fêted as a brilliant young lawyer, he'd become less and less interested in Ellie's work. Friendship and equality were things of the past. He had wanted a wife who was home when he was home, who could help him with his career and put her own work aside in deference to his.

Ellie had struggled desperately to keep on with her medicine, but by the time she had finished internship she knew it was either her medicine or her marriage. And Sam had seemed so important to her. . .

Sam had pointed out the advertisement in the *Daily*. 'You could do that,' he'd told her. 'Medical reporter. . . you write really well. That last medico-legal report you did for me was great. The pay's much better than you earn as an intern. And the hours, Ellie. . .nine to five. You could be home before me at night. I could have a cooked dinner for a change.'

He had ignored her tears, her anger and her pleading. And finally he had laid it on the line.

'I want a wife,' he had said grimly. 'And I just want a wife. I don't want a doctor.'

'We agreed to separate careers,' Ellie had protested for the hundredth time. 'We thought I'd scale down when we had children, but we have years. . .'

'That was before I realised how demanding my job would be,' Sam had told her. 'I've been asked to join the partnership of Morrison and Vernon. The partners all have wives, Ellie. Wives who entertain and keep house and support their husbands. Not doctors who stay out until all hours, come home exhausted and expect their husbands to share the workload. I want a wife, Ellie, not a doctor.'

'But I am a doctor,' Ellie had wept.

'Then you're not my wife.'

As simple as that. And Ellie had been stupid enough to concede — to throw in her precious medicine for a job writing about it. She had applied for the job at the *Daily* and got it.

Sam had been delighted.

Ellie's work at the *Daily* had chafed her to screaming-point. Her articles had been restricted to superficial issues. Any report that had threatened to interfere with the profits of large companies had been cut before it ever reached the streets.

Then, after two years — after a time that effectively stopped Ellie from re-entering the competitive medical scene — she had left work early with a migraine and arrived home to discover Sam's ultimate betrayal. She had walked out of Sam's life forever, and a week later finished at the *Daily*.

Apart from country medical practice — and Ellie felt too young and raw to try that — medicine was closed to her. Doctors didn't walk out at her stage of training and walk back in when they felt like it.

She had to do something with her life. Her mind and heart numb, she had flicked lifelessly through the medical advertisements and found Walter's. She had been medical reporter with *Our Planet's Health* ever since.

At *Our Planet's Health*, Walter bullied her unmercifully, as he did with all his staff, and paid a pittance in his efforts to keep his fledgling magazine on the streets, but he believed in what he was doing. Here, in this dilapidated old building, working with a group of people who were concerned about something other than themselves and their material possessions, Ellie had learned to gain acceptance of herself as she rebuilt her self-respect. She still missed medicine with a raw ache, but at least she felt she was doing something worthwhile.

The story of Leeton Connor's research could make the difference between this magazine continuing or going to the wall. If Ellie could pull it off. . .

'Can I have time to think about it?' she asked abruptly.

Walter gestured to the phone. 'As I said, I've already let Connor know you're coming. You've decided.'

She stared at him for a long moment, then uttered a most unladylike expletive. She stood up and walked out of Walter's office. The sound of the door slamming reverberated through the building.

'You're not really going?'

Ellie's friend Dr Laura Chang perched on Ellie's bed and stared at her friend in stupefaction. The two girls had gone through medical school together, and although their paths had diverged with Laura working at a nearby hospital as she headed for a career in child psychiatry they still remained close. Three days after Walter and Ellie's initial conversation Laura was surveying the room in awe.

'Of course I'm going.' In three days Ellie's temper had still not cooled. 'Walter Mitchen says jump and I jump. Walter Mitchen says go and spend two weeks in Antarctica with a man who hates your guts and what do I do?' She stopped her packing and spread her hands expressively. 'You see what I do?'

'But Ellie. . . Antarctica! It's even colder than here.'

Ellie raised her eyebrows in mock-surprise. 'Is it? But then I'm going prepared.' She searched the pile she was folding and threw a white garment to Laura. Laura held it up in front of her and dissolved into fits of laughter.

'Oh, Ellie, is this what the well dressed Antarcticans are wearing?' She dissolved again. 'I don't think even my grandmother would be seen dead in underwear like this.' She paused. 'Or my grandfather either, for that matter.'

Ellie grinned and reached for the offending garment. 'I have three pairs,' she confessed.

'Three pairs? How long did you say you were staying?'

'The boat should be down there for two weeks,' Ellie said seriously. 'I get off at the first port of call, at Kellent. Connor's working on Morrag, a small island just off the coast of Kellent. The ship goes along to another base further along the coast and I'll be picked up on the return journey. I gather Connor's party are coming back on the ship as well.'

'So why all the gear?' Laura frowned and leaned over to inspect Ellie's open medical bag beside the bed. 'Prepared for anything from head colds to snakebite, I see.'

'Connor's worried about one of his men,' Ellie said shortly. 'Non-specific worries, I gather; nothing for which he feels justified in ordering him to the main base for investigation. But he's worried enough to welcome a doctor.'

'Except he doesn't know it's you,' Laura said thoughtfully.

'Except he doesn't know it's me,' Ellie agreed. She

shrugged. 'I would have taken the medical supplies anyway. I'll be the only doctor on board the ship, and there's only one doctor at Kellent.'

'Well, let's hope you don't need them,' Laura said lightly. 'Removing an appendix on board an ice-breaker in a force-ten gale is not my idea of fun.'

'Because Kellent's a small settlement and isolated from the larger bases, no one's allowed there with appendix intact,' Ellie said grimly. 'I'm lucky I had mine out when I was twelve. But you're right — medical dramas are not on the agenda, as far as I'm concerned.'

'And why the rest of the gear?' Laura was fingering the piles of clothing stacked near the empty duffel bags. 'Surely for only a two-week stay. . .'

'Rules,' Ellie said shortly. 'No one goes down there unequipped for a long stay. I'll be back, though,' she said harshly. 'Even if I have to swim!'

'With the penguins and the whales,' Laura agreed sagely. 'Not that I blame you, Dr Michaels. It's hardly likely to be a romantic interlude. Now if it were me, mind. . .' She sighed. 'Not that someone like Leeton Connor would ever look twice at yours truly. With his looks and his money he only has to lift his little finger.' She grinned. 'And I don't think his little finger will crook in your direction, Dr Michaels. With the way he already feels about you, and this underwear. . .'

It was too much. She convulsed yet again in laughter. Ellie picked up a sleeping-bag and threw it at Laura's head, then went stoically on with her packing. Laura fielded the bag and surveyed her thoughtfully.

'What's he like?'

'Who?' Ellie was looking dubiously at a pair of rubber, felt-lined boots.

'Connor, of course,' Laura said patiently. 'Dr Leeton Connor, DVM.'

'Good-looking,' Ellie said shortly.

'I'm not blind,' Laura said in exasperation. 'Until he

left for the Antarctic he would have appeared on my breakfast table at least twice a week. The social columnists love him. But what's he like?'

Ellie hesitated. The image of Dr Connor rose before her, his lean, powerful body and olive-skinned good looks, his high cheekbones in an almost sculpted face and his penetrating grey eyes. When Ellie had interviewed him she had been a married woman, a woman who was supposed to be impervious to other men. And yet. . .

Despite her marriage, Leeton Connor had only to look at her with that half-serious, half-mocking expression and she had been thrown into a state of sheer physical awareness of his masculinity. It had been nothing like what she had felt for Sam.

It was as if there had been something running between them, something she could almost reach out and touch, and at times she had thought he could feel it too. Sometimes, as her questions had slowed or she had looked up from writing, she had found his eyes resting on her, enigmatic but still containing a hint of something that resembled puzzlement.

Leeton's expression, even just his presence, had left her breathless and fighting to keep sufficient composure to maintain her normally efficient interviewing techniques. Her reaction had stunned and frightened her.

It was what he did to all women, she told herself angrily, bringing herself back to the present and shoving her boots into her open bag. It was what he did to all his stable of women.

'He's an arrogant, chauvinistic womaniser,' she said harshly to Laura. 'He's just like my ex-husband. He's been pampered since birth and won't brook opposition. He nearly deserved what I did to him.'

'But not quite?' Laura prompted. Laura, like most Americans, had read the article.

Ellie hesitated and then shook her head. 'No,' she said slowly. 'Not quite.'

'So you're off to Antarctica to spend two weeks with a chauvinstic womaniser who hates your guts,' said Laura slowly. She shook her head and smiled. 'Dr Eleanor Michaels, as an almost qualified psychiatrist I have to tell you I have made a definite diagnosis. You are completely, absolutely and beyond any shadow of doubt certifiably nuts.'

CHAPTER TWO

THREE weeks later, Ellie was still agreeing with Laura's last words. Seated in the bow of the LARC — the amphibious vehicle used for unloading passengers and cargo from the *Ice Maiden* — with the biting wind on her face as the boat made its way through the slush of ice to the barren shoreline of Antarctica, she felt a surge of overwhelming panic.

For much of the journey on the *Ice Maiden* she had been able to suppress it. There had been simply too much to do and to see for her to spend time contemplating her next meeting with Leeton Connor.

She had been in demand on the ship, putting her career as journalist on hold while she was needed as a doctor. The journey had been rough, and many of the crew were suffering as well as the passengers. Ellie had good sea-legs, but even she had spent a couple of days confined to her bunk.

She had recovered to realise that many were worse off, and she had spent much of the boat's perilous passage through the 'roaring forties' and 'furious fifties' moving from bunk to bunk, dispensing sympathy and seasickness medication, and checking that fluid intakes were maintained.

As they moved closer to their destination, however, the sheer quantity of sea ice seemed to calm the heaving ocean surface, and white faces started appearing from below to gaze in wonder at this new white world. Ellie was free again to think of what was before her. Leeton Connor. When would she see him?

Now? She looked at the tiny cluster of buildings on

the rocky shoreline, with men emerging as news of the ship's arrival broke. Maybe he was here now?

It was a desolate place. The entrance to Kellent Cove seemed to be walled by icebergs packed hard against each other. Even though it was summer here, ice floated in a thick slush around the boat. On shore the ice had retreated, revealing barren mounds of exposed rock jutting from a vast, ice-covered terrain. The base buildings looked small, insignificant and defenceless.

Defenceless. Ellie considered her adjective and decided it was apt. The whole man-made settlement looked as though a decent storm or a shift of the mass of ice in the hills behind could obliterate it, leaving only a white expanse of nothing.

She sat in the boat and waited, cold and shivering despite her windproof suit. She tried to tell herself that her teeth were chattering simply from cold. As the LARC surged from the sea to roll over the rocky shore and come to rest, it was all Ellie could do not to put her head in her arms and hide herself away. She didn't want to meet Leeton Connor.

He wasn't there. A quick glance and then another. There were bearded faces around the boat, giving its occupants a noisy welcome, but Leeton Connor wasn't among them. Instead a large, red-bearded giant of a man leaned into the boat and gripped her hand.

'Dr Michaels? I'm Dr Stephen Ryde. Welcome to Kellent.'

Stephen Ryde was big and genial, twenty years older than Ellie, with a weatherbeaten face and a warm smile. He greeted Ellie with unmistakable delight.

'I know you're here as Lee Connor's journalist,' he told her, 'but I've nabbed you for a couple of hours before the LARC takes you across to Morrag.' He threw a couple of swift directions to the men unpacking Ellie's gear and then towed her up towards the desolate buildings of Kellent.

'You must feel isolated down here,' Ellie ventured, slightly breathless from her greeting.

'Bloody isolated,' he told her. 'You have no idea what it's like to be weeks from the nearest anaesthetist.'

She nodded. Stephen Ryde's story would make good material for *Our Planet's Health*. Not as sensational as Connor's but almost as interesting.

'How do you manage?' she asked him.

He shrugged, leading the way through what seemed a rabbit warren of buildings. 'Some of the expeditioners undertake anaesthetic training before they came down here. Rough, but I use 'em if I have to. For a real emergency I use your Dr Connor. He's an able vet — a damned skilled man.'

Ellie's brow furrowed. Surely this was not a description of the man she had interviewed two years ago?

'We had a nasty accident a couple of months back,' Dr Ryde was saying. 'Couple of men in a snowmobile — hit a spot of blue ice and went into a slide. They were able to jump out, but one of them broke two ankles and a few other bones. I had to reduce the fractures, and doing that sort of job with a plumber who's done a weekend's training in anaesthetics is no joke.' He grinned. 'Lee came over, figured out what the man was equivalent to in animals — slightly less than a horse, I gather — and we went from there. Worked like a charm.' He smiled at Ellie. 'All the same, my dear, it's good to have you here.'

'What happened to the patient?' Ellie asked curiously. 'If you had to reduce the fractures he'd need rehabilitation. . .'

'We got him out,' Dr Ryde reassured her. 'We flew him by helicopter to the Russian base, transferred him to a Russian ship which took him via the Antarctic Peninsula to Argentina. He was home in a fortnight.'

He hesitated then shrugged. 'Bit of a bad time for me,' he confessed. 'He had a couple of broken ribs as well, and one punctured his lung. He should have had a doctor with him every inch of the way, but there was no one who could go with him. Still, I gather he's OK now.'

'Has that been the worst of your traumas for the year?' Ellie asked. They had arrived in Dr Ryde's surgery. Fascinated, she was checking the vast array of equipment he stored in such a tiny place.

'No.' He turned and motioned out of the window at the white hillside. Against the white of the ice was a stark black cross. 'We had a perforated abscess in midwinter. One of Lee's men, actually. They were out on a field trip—there's some talk of building an airstrip smack across the breeding path of the emperor penguins and they were out building temporary barricades to assess the consequences—and Mannering collapsed. They got him back here and we operated, but it was no damned good. We needed specialist surgeons, an intensive care ward—everything we didn't have.' He shook his head. 'Lee took it hard.'

Ellie shook her head. Leeton Connor as a concerned human being? Here again was a facet of the man she hadn't known existed.

'Dr Connor's worried about another of his men, I gather,' she said slowly. 'Do you know about it?'

Dr Ryde nodded. 'I know. And there's not a lot I can do, because he won't come over to base. Gordon Fraser. He's concerned I'll stop him working and he's due to leave with the rest of Connor's team, on the *Ice Maiden*'s return journey.'

'What's wrong with him?'

'I haven't seen him since Lee's team left for Morrag at the beginning of summer. Lee tells me he's losing weight and is coughing.' The big man shrugged. 'It could be nothing. It could be stress—people react to isolation in different ways, and Fraser was very upset over Mannering's death. But Lee's worried, and if you weren't coming he'd be bringing the team back to base early.'

'The whole team?' Ellie said, startled. 'That seems a bit extreme.'

'There's only three in the team now,' Dr Ryde explained. 'And that's the minimum number for a field party. If one gets into trouble there's one to stay put while the other goes for help.' He shrugged. 'Anyway, I hope Lee's worrying for nothing. Mannering's death has made us all edgy. Let me know when you see him.'

The rest of Ellie's time at Kellent passed quickly. After lunch in a crowded mess Dr Ryde escorted her down to the beach where the LARC was packed and ready for the short trip to Morrag. Ellie wished him farewell with reluctance. In this short time it seemed she had made a friend. She was under no illusion that any friendship was waiting for her at Morrag.

An hour later, after a rough trip in the small boat, the rocky outcrop of Morrag came into view. Ellie was apprehensive enough, but as the crew produced a small, inflatable dinghy and proceeded not only to launch it but to stow her baggage into it she was horrified.

'I don't have to get into that thing?' she gasped.

'You must,' the man at the helm told her. 'Morrag is a specially protected area. We have to obtain special permission for even these small boats to land here.'

'Good grief!' The knot of apprehension in Ellie's stomach was tightening with each moment. The men laughed sympathetically and she was handed a huge red rubber suit. She looked at it with dismay.

'Do I have to wear this? I'm warm enough already.'

'You wouldn't be if you fell in,' she was told severely. 'This is an immersion suit. If you fell into this water you'd die in minutes. The water here is almost freezing.'

Ellie put on the suit.

Despite her fears, the twenty-minute trip was uneventful and the huge red suit was unnecessary. The knot of panic as her meeting with Leeton Connor grew closer was tightening with every moment, but even her tension could not lessen the wonder of what she was experiencing.

There were birds everywhere. The water was alive with black and white torpedoes — penguins searching for food to satisfy their chicks. Somewhere on Morrag Island was a rookery where hundreds of fluffy, fat chicks would be waiting for these torpedoes to return with dinner.

Also floating past the boat were fat Weddell seals, lolling lazily on the ice-floes. At any other time Ellie would have been enthralled, but as she lifted her camera to take yet another photograph the boat turned into a cove where red, apple-shaped domes on the shore denoted the presence of a campsite. Ellie could make out the figure standing on the shore. Even at this distance she recognised the man she had travelled half a world to interview.

As they approached the shore Leeton Connor was knee-high in the water, protected from the sea by thick rubber waders, waiting to lift the boat from the water. The wind was rising and, even in the protected cove, the sea was becoming distinctly unfriendly.

He knew who she was. One glance up as they touched the shore told Ellie that Leeton Connor had discovered, before her arrival, that Dr Eleanor Coad and Dr Ellie Michaels were the same person. His face was harsh and judgemental, but there was no trace of shock.

Ellie felt her spirits sink at the sight of his uncompromising countenance. He was thinner than she remembered, and his face had been weathered by a year in this harsh climate. He was still clean-shaven. In this society of bearded males it seemed almost odd. A beard on

Leeton Connor would be a frightening thing, she thought grimly; his face was black enough already. He helped Ellie out of the boat without comment and then turned back to help the crew member from the LARC to remove her belongings.

The man looked uncertainly from Leeton to Ellie. 'Dr Connor,' he started uncertainly, 'this is. . .'

'I know who this is.' Leeton's tone was uncompromising. 'This is Eleanor Coad, whatever name she may be calling herself, and for whatever reason——'

'It's Michaels,' Ellie broke in, forcing herself to speak. She smiled at the man from the LARC. 'Dr Connor and I have met before, in New York, while I was using another name.' She took a deep breath and turned her bright smile on to Leeton. 'Aren't you going to welcome me ashore, Dr Connor?'

He eyed her grimly. 'Whatever you may be calling yourself, there's no welcome here for you,' he said harshly. 'You've a job to do. Let's get on with it.' He bent and lifted one side of the dinghy ready for relaunch and signalled to the other man to do the same. 'You'd best get this thing back out to the LARC before the weather turns against you.'

Two minutes later the boat was back in the water, and Ellie's last link with the mainland was disappearing. She was left alone with Leeton Connor.

He ignored her. After relaunching the boat he simply turned back, picked up a couple of her bags and started walking up the rocky shoreline towards the camp. Ellie was left, still struggling to free herself from the cumbersome immersion suit.

Her face was almost as red as the suit, both from exertion and humiliation. She had asked for this treatment. Somehow she had to keep quiet, ignore Leeton Connor's anger and get the job done. Finally free of the bulky clothing, she gathered her remaining belongings and started over the rocks after him.

The huts, at close quarters, still resembled apples, with their bottom third cut away. They stood about eight feet high and maybe ten feet in diameter, with portholes acting as windows. They were nestled on a rocky ledge about fifty feet above the sea, secured to the ground by metal cables. The wind whipping around them was making the cables hum. Apart from the cry of the birds it was the only sound in what was otherwise an almost eerie quiet.

Leeton Connor had pulled back the door of the nearest hut and passed Ellie's bags inside. He stood at the open door and waited for her to struggle up the rocks towards him. As she neared the hut another figure, a blond, bearded hulk with a welcoming smile, appeared from above the ridge and swung himself down to take her burden from her.

'I'm Sven Benner,' he smiled at her, and his warm blue eyes were definitely welcoming. 'I am sorry Gordon and I were not here to greet you, but the weather will break soon, and we have much to do before that happens.'

His accent was Swedish, Ellie decided. She smiled back at him, absurdly comforted by his welcome.

'Hi,' she said stupidly.

Sven lifted her remaining belongings and handed them over to Leeton Connor to pass inside the hut. His smile slipped and he frowned.

'Lee, are you sure about this? You know we can make room for you with us. Gordon and I can pack away some equipment.'

Leeton shook his head. He smiled, but the smile didn't reach his eyes. 'Thanks, Sven. It's good of you to offer, but we needn't put you out, need we, Dr Coad? Dr Coad's boss has explained that we're not to go to any trouble because she's a female. Isn't that right, Dr Coad?'

Ellie gasped as the implications of their words hit home. She would be sharing a hut with Leeton Connor!

He was watching her, waiting for her protest. She looked up and caught amusement lurking in the deep eyes. Her anger rose and came to her aid. This man was not going to humiliate her as easily as he so obviously expected.

'My name,' she repeated icily, 'is Dr Ellie Michaels. I no longer respond to Coad and would prefer you to remember that, Dr Connor.' She smiled in a tightly defiant expression of pride. 'And of course I wouldn't want to put you out.' She forced a little more warmth into her voice as she addressed Sven. 'I'm here to do my job and inconvenience you as little as possible.'

'Well, if that's settled,' Leeton Connor said smoothly, 'maybe we can leave Dr Coad. . .' He paused and then corrected himself with exaggerated care. 'Maybe we can leave Dr Michaels to stow her gear while we take care of dinner.' He held the door of the little red hut and waited for her to enter. His eyes mocked her as she brushed past. The door closed and she was left alone.

For a moment Ellie stood absolutely still. Her face burned. Her whole body wanted to cringe into a mortified speck of something that could blend into this white landscape and disappear.

How could she cope with a man who had not forgotten or forgiven but who had clearly decided to use the opportunity of her presence here to exact a calculated revenge?

Somehow she was going to have to break through his barrier of icy contempt, apologise and explain the reasons which had driven her to write that accursed article. Somehow she had to create a working relationship with this man.

She looked down, and her breath caught in her throat. The tiny hut was ordered and neat, with everything in its place. Leeton Connor's scientific equipment took up much of the space, but it had obviously been reorganised to allow two bunks to lie side by side.

Ellie was caught and held by sheer panic. Laura's words came floating back, and she knew with surety that they had been absolutely correct. Eleanor Michaels had, indeed, taken leave of her senses.

CHAPTER THREE

IT WAS a stressful meal that night. They ate in Sven and Gordon's hut. Sven cooked in what Ellie assumed was his turn at a strict roster. She guessed she would be expected to take turns like the others, but for tonight she was being treated like a guest.

At least, she was by Sven and Gordon. They were delighted to have a visitor, but Leeton's reaction was clearly puzzling them. They tried to make up for his coolness with light-hearted banter, but his icy indifference and the tension in Ellie put a damper on the whole group. As the meal progressed, Ellie found herself more and more angry at Leeton Connor's blatant contempt.

Gordon, lean, tall and bearded, had returned from his visit to the breeding grounds of the skuas as the wind rose. As Leeton's ill humour became increasingly obvious, Gordon attempted to fill the awkward silence by haltingly telling Ellie about his day's work.

She had already seen the skuas in her short time at Kellent and had decided they were not her favourite of the Antarctic birds. Natural predators, they lived on eggs and young of other birds, plus any rubbish and carcasses they could scavenge with their strong curved beaks. They bred on a flat peak above the camp at Morrag.

Despite her aversion to the birds, Ellie listened with interest to Gordon's halting explanation of the birds' feeding and mating habits. She had no doubt she would be climbing the peak to photograph these birds before she left, although what she had read of them suggested they were not averse to attack on humans if they seemed threatening to nesting sites.

The skuas could wait. Of more immediate concern to her at the moment was Gordon himself. She had heard concerns about this man's health, and the reason was obvious.

The man looked ill. His halting speech was partly a product of shyness, Ellie realised, but also there was an element of effort, as if he could not take enough air into his lungs to complete a long sentence. His frame was thin, almost to the point of emaciation, and his hands shook as they lifted fork and knife. His complexion too... Ellie watched him covertly as he talked and decided she would dearly like a barrage of blood tests. Was the man anaemic? And if he was, what was causing it?

He ate half as much as the other men, and even that seemed an effort. Could it be stress and isolation? Stephen Ryde's words came back to her and she turned them over in her mind. Depression and isolation did strange things to people. If Gordon was too depressed to eat, problems could compound themselves.

'Do you and Sven have family back home?' she asked cautiously. She cast a nervous glance at Leeton, silently watching from the other side of the hut. 'I know Dr Connor's a bachelor. How about you?'

'Checking the field, are we, Dr Michaels?' Leeton's sardonic drawl made Ellie flush crimson and she bit her lip.

Sven cast a look of surprise at his boss before answering her. There was something going on that he didn't understand, and he clearly didn't like it.

'I have a wife and two little girls,' he told Ellie gently, trying to drive the distress from her eyes. 'Gordon has only his parents and five sisters and thirteen nephews and nieces.'

'Goodness!' Ellie attempted a laugh. 'You must miss them.'

'It may come as a surprise to you, but some of us can do without the social whirl,' Leeton drawled.

It was no use continuing with this farce. Ellie dredged up a smile and rose from the table.

'I'm afraid you'll have to excuse me.' She smiled stiffly at Sven and Gordon. Her smile carefully excluded Leeton. 'I'm really very tired. I'll leave you to finish your coffee in peace.' She shrugged. 'Maybe Dr Connor will find something pleasant to say, with me gone.' She donned her anorak and headed back out into the wind.

As the door closed behind her she heard Sven's voice raised in expostulation. She smiled humourlessly. Let Leeton explain his boorish manners away, she thought bitterly. He couldn't. His conduct had been appalling.

It was late, but it still was not near dark. Already, though, Ellie was adjusting to sleeping in daylight. At this time of the year if she were to sleep only in darkness she would be getting no more than a couple of hours' sleep a night. At least there were those two blessed hours of darkness. If she had been here in midsummer there would have been none.

There was a tiny hut specifically designated a bathroom, although it was also used for storing equipment. Ellie investigated, and decided her personal hygiene was going to be less than perfect for the length of her stay on Morrag. Shovelling snow into an ice-melter before showering was hardly her idea of fun. She gave a thankful little prayer for her forethought in having only half a cup of coffee with her dinner. To have to bundle up and brave this in the middle of the night would be horrific.

With her sketchy ablutions done, she once more faced the wind and made her way back to the hut she and Leeton were going to occupy.

He had not returned. Swiftly Ellie undressed, cringing at the bitter cold on her naked skin. She pulled on a soft nightshirt to protect her shoulders from the draughts through the top of her bag, then slid into the sleeping-bag's thick cocoon of down.

She was weary; bone-tired from both exertion and stress. She wished the light would fade, but she knew that darkness would not bring sleep.

Gordon. . . Concentrate on Gordon, she told herself. What was wrong with the man?

No wonder Leeton was concerned. There had to be some underlying cause — some problem causing weight loss and debility. It was so hard, because she had nothing to go on. Had he been thin before he had come down here, or had that gaunt, half-starved appearance occurred dramatically over the last few weeks?

She shook her head into the half-light. Leeton Connor was just going to have to talk to her if he wanted her to do anything.

He was going to have to talk to her if she was to give him the publicity he needed. The whole thing was crazy. If he intended sending her to Coventry for her whole stay she might just as well have remained in New York.

It was another hour before Ellie finally heard the sound of the hut's metal door swinging open. She was wide awake, but she lay with her face to the wall, feigning sleep. Leeton's bunk was so close that she could feel him settling into his bag, his movements making her bunk stir slightly. It was like being in a double bed, she thought with horror.

'Dr Connor?'

She forced the words out. There was no way she could sleep with this tension between them. Somehow she had to talk to him. If she was goig to lie awake for the rest of the night then that talk might as well be now. She stayed turned away, though. To turn over and face him would bring her face within an arm's reach of his, and she couldn't bear it.

'Yes?' The voice was polite and impersonal.

'This is crazy.' Ellie's voice was not quite steady.

'As you say.' Leeton's agreement was totally uninterested.

She took a deep breath, striving for calm. 'How long has Gordon being losing weight?' she asked finally. It seemed the safest topic she could think of.

'I don't think Gordon's health need concern you,' Leeton said brutally. 'He's not so ill that he needs some semi-qualified medico gossip columnist prying into what's none of her business.'

Ellie closed her eyes. The tension within her was building to the point where she was no longer in control. 'Why did you agree to my coming if you knew who I was?' she asked tightly.

'Why should that possibly interest you?' His voice was calm. 'You got here. Isn't that enough?'

'No, it's not enough.' Ellie swung around in her narrow bed—then wished she hadn't. Leeton's deep grey eyes were watching her coolly from a pillow's width away. 'You've agreed to these articles for *Our Planet's Health*,' she made herself continue. 'They're important, for you, for our magazine and maybe even for this continent. Now I arrive and I find you have nothing more to say to me than you absolutely must. You're still nursing a petty grievance over something I wrote two years ago, for another newspaper and for another purpose.'

'And that purpose?' Leeton's eyes, in the dim half-light, were still and expressionless.

Ellie bit her lip. It went against the grain, but she was going to have to do it. 'I'm sorry,' she said softly. 'I owe you an apology for that article. It was written when I shouldn't have been working. I was angry and upset about something personal, and I took it out on you.'

'So why wait until now to apologise?'

'I'm apologising for the tone of the article,' Ellie said quietly. 'Nothing more. My facts were accurate.'

'As far as they went they were accurate,' Leeton said harshly. 'Deception by omission, I believe it's called. Giving an overview of my life and my career, with four pages on my social life and two paragraphs on my academic achievements.'

'It seemed to me your social life was your major interest,' Ellie snapped.

'And that's what your muck-raking mind wanted to believe. That's what the *Daily* readers wanted to hear,' Leeton said coldly. 'So you gave it to them, with both barrels. Every piece of sordid gossip that's ever been whispered about me, in truth or in jealousy. And you still believe I keep—how did you put it?—a stable of horses, a stable of cars and a stable of women?'

'I've no idea what you now possess,' Ellie snapped. 'I dare say when you get this little jaunt out of the way you'll return to your pampered lifestyle——'

'But for now?' he broke in. 'Where are my horses, Dr Coad? Or my cars?' He shook his head. 'What makes you think I can survive without the things you say I'm dependent on? And my women?' He smiled, a bitter half-smile. 'Your article questioned what sort of man I would be, stripped of the wealth I'd inherited.' He paused, then went on, his voice not losing its implacable bitterness, 'You asked why I permitted you to come. Maybe it's true I can't live without my women. Maybe even Dr Eleanor Coad is better than no woman at all.'

He reached a muscled arm out. His hand slipped into the hood of her bag and he pulled her face towards him. Ellie pulled back in horror, but his movements were inexorable. She fought to get her hands free of the encumbering bag, but he was too swift. Her face was close against his; his mouth was searching for hers.

It was a cruel kiss, harsh, searching and demanding. His lips enveloped hers, his tongue demanding an entry. As her mouth opened with the force of his pressure, his hand slid down into the warm recess of her bag to feel the contours of her rigid body. He pulled her hard against him, her body, still in its imprisoning cocoon of a sleeping-bag, being held and lifted almost completely on to the narrowness of Leeton's bunk.

She pulled back with all her strength, fighting against the demanding forces of this man's hands. It was futile. Ellie was slightly built and this man, with his superbly muscled body and his iron will, had the strength to overpower most men of his own size. She had no defence.

Finally she lay passively against him, trying to block what was being done to her, trying to block the feel of this ruthless male body against hers — trying to block the errant quiver of response she felt her body make.

It was there. Try as she might to ignore it, her body betrayed her. From the time she had first met Leeton Connor her body had responded with physical arousal. She knew it, she thought bleakly, even though she had not acknowledged it to herself before this moment. The feel of his hands against the soft curve of her back sent tremors of awareness through her, demanding a response.

His hands searched to find an edge to the soft cloth of her shirt. Lifting it, they moved to finger her breasts, roughly caressing the soft flesh. Her nipples responded to his touch, betraying the war that was occurring within her. Not since Sam had a man touched her so, and even with Sam. . .

The thought of her husband and the pain he had inflicted on her was enough to give Ellie added strength. With tears streaming down her face she fought to free a hand and shoved with all the strength she possessed. As Leeton's grip broke momentarily, she pulled herself back, crouching against the wall like a terrified animal.

'Leave me alone.' It was a desperate whisper.

Leeton relinquished his hold. He lay back on his

pillow, watching her sardonically. 'Why don't you scream for help?'

Outside the wind was building to almost gale force. No sound of Ellie's would have made itself heard above it.

'Would you rape me?' she asked shakily. 'Would you rape me for revenge? Have I hurt you enough to warrant that?'

There was silence between them, broken only by the roar of the wind and the deep humming of the steel cables holding their little hut secure.

'Why did you use a false name?' he asked finally, seemingly at a tangent to what had just occurred between them. 'Did you think I wouldn't find out? Even if I hadn't bothered to research your background, I would have known the moment you got off the boat.' His eyes hadn't moved from her face.

'I didn't try to deceive you,' she said defensively. 'My boss used my real name when he told you I was coming.'

'And you change names whenever you change jobs?'

'No. Whenever I change husbands,' she said bitterly.

His hand reached out and gripped hers, pulling it to inspect the third finger of her left hand.

'Your husband?' His tone was suddenly unsure.

'I don't have one,' she responded quietly, withdrawing her hand with an effort. 'I did when I worked for the *Daily*.' She hesitated then forced herself to explain. 'The day before my last interview with you I discovered he was having an affair with another woman. I took a lot of bitterness out on you, and I'm sorry.' She took a deep breath. 'It doesn't warrant this treatment, though.'

Leeton's face was unreadable in the deepening gloom. 'So Dr Eleanor Coad was reacting with hate to all men when she wrote that article.'

'Please. . .' Ellie's tears were still sliding unchecked down her face. 'Please, I'm Ellie Michaels. I haven't been Ellie Coad for years.' Her voice was suddenly vehement. 'Like you, I hate Ellie Coad. Can't we forget what I did, what I've been before? Can't we just get this job done and go our separate ways? Are you so small-minded that you can't forgive a slight?'

'A slight published in eight languages for a readership of millions?' Leeton asked incredulously.

'I. . . I've said I'm sorry.'

'And that's supposed to be enough?'

There was a long silence. Ellie stayed where she was, crouched against the cold metal of the hut wall. She was aware that she was shaking. She pulled her bag up around her, seeking the comfort of its warmth. She had never felt so desolate; so alone. This man made her feel worthless, a subhuman member of the species. The horrible thing was that she knew she deserved it. A violent shudder passed through her.

He was still watching her. Her tremor was obvious. He shook his head impatiently.

'You can stop panicking, Dr Michaels.' His tone was almost gentle. 'I'm not about to rape you, whatever you may believe me capable of.' He sank down against his pillow and considered her. 'I still don't know why you're here. If I'd known who you were before you left I would have prevented you from coming, and you must have known that. Unfortunately the response to my query on your background was delayed until it was too late.'

He paused and turned to lie on his back, staring up at the roof. 'This work is important to me, Ellie. Whatever lies you've printed in the past, this is my life's work, and you'll not interfere with it. It's vital that it receives the media coverage it deserves. If I'm stuck with you for that coverage, then I have to make the most of it.' His tone went suddenly harsh. 'But, by God, it had better be good. I don't care about the reason you came. You can forget it. What's in front of you is two of the hardest weeks you've known, and me looking over your shoulder every inch of the way. And if you don't get it right. . .'

He paused and then said smoothly, 'But that's not going to happen, is it, Dr Michaels? This is going to be the best damn coverage you've ever produced in your life.' He turned over, pulled the hood of his bag and concentrated on sleep.

Ellie finally managed some sleep. Not much, but enough. Exhaustion finally took over from the turmoil of emotions crowding in her tired brain.

When she woke, Leeton was up and dressed. He was moving around the tiny hut, preparing breakfast. As she opened her eyes he came towards her, carrying a mug of steaming coffee. His tall body, clad in serviceable trousers and a bulky woollen sweater, towered above her. She sat up, pulling the bag with her. He eyed her defensive measures with amusement.

'Still on your guard, Dr Michaels? Very wise.'

Ellie glared at him and took the coffee, cupping it in both hands to gain warmth from its heat. The temperature outside her bag was freezing. Her hands were already losing their colour with the cold.

'I suggest you dress before you tackle this.' Leeton motioned towards the eggs and bacon he was cooking.

'I. . . I don't normally eat breakfast,' Ellie said.

'Here you do,' he said curtly. 'It's freezing and you have a hard day's physical work in front of you. You can't do that on a cup of black coffee.' He waited until she had drained her cup, took it from her and turned back to the Primus stove. 'Now, get dressed.'

'Here?' She said the word with dismay. He didn't turn back.

'Dr Michaels, if you think I'm staying outside in a temperature of ten below freezing with another twenty or thirty degrees off for wind chill just so you can get dressed with modesty, you can think again. Now, I'm standing in front of this stove looking at it, not you, for another minute and a half. Ninety seconds. If I were you, I'd move.'

Ellie moved.

Dressed and breakfasted, she made a dash for the 'bathroom'. She came back subdued, white with cold.

'Lesson number one,' Leeton said drily as she re-entered the hut. 'If there's any wind at all you don't even stick your nose out of this door without all your protective clothing.' He took one of her hands into his. It was bloodless and freezing. 'Including your gloves.'

It was the first of many lessons Ellie was to learn. In her time working for *Our Planet's Health* she had travelled to many of the earth's more remote and inaccessible areas, and none had seemed so totally forbidding as this place.

It wasn't meant for human habitation, Ellie thought, staring through her porthole at the bleak landscape. Leeton was in the other hut discussing plans for the day with Sven and Gordon, and Ellie was trying to put her jumbled impressions on paper. Leeton was right in the attitude he presented to the world, she decided. Man had no place here. This place belonged to the animals who had somehow evolved with the ability to survive here.

As the morning progressed, the wind dropped and she ventured from the comparative warmth of the tiny hut to marvel at the sheer bleakness of their campsite. Its very bleakness was a source of spectacular beauty. Even now, at the end of summer, ice remained over many of the rocks forming the island. Down at the shoreline the rocks were exposed, but where the ice had formed deeper layers the melt had not extended to the base. The larger rock formations appeared grey and worn, as if they had grown from a bed of white. Tiny lichen and moss patches appeared in some of the more sheltered areas of rock. That was the total vegetation of the island.

Ellie walked down to the shore and looked back up to the tiny camp. This was home for the next two weeks. Bundled up against the bitter chill, she felt her spirits lift. The dreaded meeting with Leeton Connor had taken place and she was still alive to tell the tale. Somehow maybe the tensions between the two of them could be shelved and she could get on with documenting his work on this magic place.

For magic it was. The weak sun was doing its best to be warm, and the ice in the sunlight was glistening pure white. Ellie had never seen such a white. She half closed her eyes in defence against its glare, rejecting at the same time Leeton's advice to wear goggles. When working with her cameras the goggles were an impossibility, and besides, she wanted to see this place as it really was.

The men had emerged a few minutes before her. Around the headland she could see them crouched, setting up equipment on a rocky outcrop that seemed alive with birds. Ellie shaded her eyes with her hand to make out Leeton rising and coming towards her. He had seen her emerge. She stood still while he strode easily over the rocks to greet her.

'Good afternoon,' he said mockingly, and she flushed. It was still just a little after nine.

'I had to write up my notes from yesterday,' she said defensively, and he raised his eyebrows.

'Of course,' he agreed, in a tone that made her want to hit him.

'What are you doing today?' she asked through gritted teeth.

'Banding petrels.' Still the icy courtesy was maintained. 'Would you like a ringside seat?'

Ellie bit her lip. 'I'd like to help, if I could,' she said

tightly. 'It gives me a much better feel to your work if I can be involved.'

Again he raised his eyebrows as if the thought of Dr Ellie Michaels doing any physical work was ridiculous. 'Of course,' he agreed politely, and Ellie's slapping fingers itched.

'Tell me about Gordon,' she forced herself to say. She hesitated. 'Look, I've been disparaging of your veterinary skills in the past and you've been disparaging of my medical skills. The truth is that I'm a qualified doctor. I'm still registered and my skills are still up to date.'

He was looking at her strangely. 'But you chose to abandon medicine,' he said slowly.

'It wasn't my choice.'

'Then why. . .?'

'For reasons that have nothing to do with you,' she told him. 'But I'm still a doctor. A doctor with a different role.' She took a deep breath, trying to make him see how important medicine still was to her. 'Like you,' she continued. 'Your aim is to preserve wildlife, yet you're still a vet. It doesn't make you less of a vet just because you no longer treat sick poodles.'

He smiled, and for the first time Ellie caught a glimpse of warmth. 'I could still treat a sick poodle,' he said firmly. 'Despite what your article implied.'

She thought back to what Stephen Ryde had told her about this man. 'He's an able vet — a damned skilled man.'

'I know you could.' She said the words reluctantly and her voice fell away. 'I'm starting to know that.'

The wind had totally disappeared. The only sound was the faint lapping of the waves at the shoreline, but even that was muted. The sheer bulk of sea ice floating around the cove made it impossible for the waves to build. Ellie stood looking at the tip of her rubber-booted foot against the slate-grey rock. Leeton looked down at her, as if trying to read from her bowed head just who he was dealing with.

'OK, Dr Michaels,' he said quietly, as if he had come to some decision, 'I would like you to try and find out what's wrong with Gordon.'

Ellie nodded. 'How long has he been losing weight?'

'He was thin to begin with,' Leeton said, considering. 'It's been so gradual that it's really only for the past three weeks that I've been concerned. He collapsed on the way back from a field trip. Not significantly — half an hour's rest and he was right to continue — but it was enough to make me take a really close look at him, and I didn't like what I saw.'

Ellie nodded. 'So why didn't you send him over to Dr Ryde at Kellent?'

'Do you think I didn't try?' He shrugged. 'He says he simply had a heavy cold — which is true — and it's put him off his food. Now he agrees he won't fully recover until we leave, but with only a fortnight to go he has no intention of finishing early.' Leeton shrugged again. 'I'd probably do the same thing myself, but now the worry's embedded I can't look at the man without imagining there's something more serious than just the flu.' He frowned down at Ellie. 'Did Steve Ryde tell you about Mannering?'

'Yes.'

He shrugged. 'Then you'll probably guess my concern. I've already lost one of my men.'

'You couldn't possibly have anticipated a perforated ulcer,' Ellie said quickly.

'Maybe not.' His hands were dug deep in his pockets and his eyes were not seeing her. 'But I was so caught up in the work we were doing I wasn't looking for the signs. Maybe if I'd been looking, Mannering would be alive today.'

'And probably he wouldn't,' Ellie said gently. 'He was young and fit and was probably asymptomatic.

Besides. . .' she attempted a smile '. . .you couldn't possibly have known what to look for. Poodles don't have ulcers.'

The man beside her raised his eyebrows. 'Don't they?' he said mockingly. 'The oh, so knowledgeable Dr Michaels has just made a major medical blunder. Poodles get gastric ulcers just the same as humans. It's less likely because they're not as prone to putting beer in their stomachs as their human counterparts, but give me a highly strung poodle fed table scraps and chocolate doggy treats and I'll show you a candidate for a stomach ulcer.'

'I beg your pardon, I'm sure,' Ellie said stiffly. 'My medical training must have been sadly remiss not to have included that piece of vital information.'

Leeton grinned. Then he looked over to where Sven and Gordon were working though and his smile faded.

'Does Gordon?' he asked.

'Have an ulcer?' She looked up, startled. 'I wouldn't think an ulcer would be causing this gradual weight loss. It's one of the less likely causes.'

'Then what?'

She spread her hands helplessly. 'For heaven's sake, Dr Connor, competent I might be, but I'm not omnipotent. He's lost weight. He seems debilitated and he looks anaemic. I'd like a white cell count.'

Leeton frowned. 'Leukaemia?'

Ellie shook her head. 'You're dredging up worst case scenarios, Dr Connor. The answer is that I don't know. The only way you could have known Mannering had a stomach ulcer was if he was to tell you he was suffering discomfort. And there's little I can do if Gordon won't confide in me. Your alternative is to pack him over to Kellent and order a complete physical examination.'

Leeton nodded. 'I understand that,' he said heavily. 'It's not what Gordon wants and it's not what I want. See what you can do without that.'

There was a moment's silence, then Leeton sighed. For a moment Ellie had an almost overwhelming impression that the pressures on this man's shoulders were too heavy for him to bear. Then he looked over to where Sven and Gordon were working in the midst of a squawking, wheeling cacophony of birds.

'OK, Dr Michaels,' he said firmly. 'Let's put you to work.'

CHAPTER FOUR

SVEN and Gordon looked up as they approached and greeted Ellie easily. They were working at a nesting site. The rocky ledges were littered with nesting birds, dedicated to their eggs and chicks.

This dedication was almost total. The birds didn't stir as humans approached. If Ellie failed to move with care she would have stood on eggs, chicks or even parent birds. With their lack of natural enemies, the birds showed no fear. Their only danger to their eggs and chicks was the skuas, and generations of birds had learned to react to danger by staying with chick or egg.

Ellie stood for a few moments as the men talked, wondering at the toughness of these birds to be able to nest in such a place. It was bare rock, with no nesting material apart from ice and rock.

'Watch for a few moments,' Leeton told her as he knelt to start work. 'When you're familiar with the technique you can do some yourself.'

Ellie needed no further prodding. Already her camera was raised. The men were catching the birds with their gloved hands. Unused to predators, the birds were easy to catch. Each bird was gently placed into a tapered bag while it was weighed, measured for head, wing and bill length and its number of tail and flight feathers counted. It was then banded and released.

The birds didn't seem unduly bothered by their ordeal. As the dark-streaked Antarctic petrels were released they didn't fly off immediately. Instead they seated themselves carefully on the rock as if to compose themselves before flying off out of reach.

'You're lucky we're doing the Antarctic petrels,' Sven

told Ellie as he flipped another bird expertly into its
bag. 'The snow petrels have a charming defence mech-
anism. They spit their stomach contents; a lovely fishy
oily substance that stinks like. . .like. . .'

'Like half-digested fish,' Gordon suggested, and they
all laughed at Ellie's expression of disgust.

'Tell me why you're doing this?' She asked the
question as she moved around quietly with her camera.

She addressed Gordon, but was not surprised when
he didn't answer. Gordon seemed nervous of her, and
shy. Was it the fact that he had been in an isolated
group for over twelve months, Ellie wondered, or was it
something else? In the end Leeton answered.

'There are nesting sites for these birds both here and
on the mainland,' he told her. 'We're making comparative studies of the flocks here, where they've been
relatively undisturbed, and the flocks on the mainland,
nearer the bases.'

'Is there an obvious difference?' Ellie asked curiously.
She sounded almost hopeful, and the men laughed.

'You're hoping for birds with two heads?' Leeton
asked. 'It's hardly reached that stage. With the excep-
tion of the proposed construction of an airstrip, most of
the bases are doing their best to see that the wildlife is
undisturbed. Although, when you see the skuas brows-
ing on Kellent garbage dump, it makes you wonder.'

'So there's no real danger?'

'I didn't say that.' Leeton carefully removed the bag
from the bird he had just banded. The bird cast him an
indignant look before seating itself carefully on the rock
beside him. You don't scare me, it seemed to be saying.
Then, honour satisfied, it spread its wings and flew out
to sea.

'All these birds need this type of ground for breeding,'
Leeton continued, his dark eyes narrowing as he
watched the bird wheel around the headland. 'Rocky
shoreline, free from ice. Antarctica has about eighteen

thousand miles of shoreline. Of that, only about three hundred are ice-free in summer. What we have now is humans and birds competing for the space. Not forgetting the seals,' he added.

Ellie caught her breath. 'Only three hundred miles?'

'That's all,' he confirmed. 'And when you have every interested nation determined not only to have a base down here but also wanting airstrips and sometimes even tourist facilities, then the problem becomes a major one.'

'But there's no problem here,' Ellie said slowly, as if reassuring herself. She looked around at the mass of birdlife surrounding them.

'No, not here. What we're doing, though, is trying to assess whether this colony of birds is building up in response to the pressures on the mainland.'

She stared around them. It seemed impossible that this barren, untouched land could be threatened.

The sun glistened on the ice-strewn sea. The wind was almost non-existent. Down on the water a group of seals were lolling on ice-floes, as if they had nothing to do in the world but to enjoy the sun.

'Pups,' Leeton said, following her gaze. 'The harsh realities of an Antarctic winter haven't hit home yet.'

Ellie nodded, but as she did the idyllic scene below her was disturbed. The thin floe holding the seals was tipped as a weight was thrust underneath. The pups slid into the sea and disappeared.

The petrels were forgotten as Ellie and the three men stared down.

'It's a leopard seal,' Leeton said grimly.

Ellie stared, horrified, as the water surrounding the floe turned crimson. Blood-stained water washed back over the ice, stark and unmistakable against the pure white.

'A leopard seal. . .' she whispered. She'd read of them. They were aggressive, carnivorous and dangerous as sharks. There had even been instances of leopard seals attacking men through layers of sea ice.

'I didn't think they attacked other seals,' she whispered.

'Not their own kind,' Leeton told her. 'The pups are crab-eaters — the most common seal down here and the main prey of the leopard seal.'

'And I've seen this animal before,' Gordon said. 'He's an old bull. He sits at the entrance to the cove, watching everything that goes in and out. Any seal or penguin venturing in is fair game.'

Ellie closed her eyes. Pieces of ripped flesh were floating to the surface as the leopard seal demolished its prey. It's the natural order of things, she told herself. When she opened her eyes again she still felt sick.

Then her eyes widened. On the rocks beneath them a seal pup was dragging itself out of the water. It slid over the rocks and collapsed, exhausted, just below their ledge. From where she sat she could see a gaping tear to its side.

'The one that got away,' Gordon said grimly.

Ellie didn't hear. She was already sliding down the rocks to the injured seal.

The seal pup had been slashed along its side, and the ragged tear was bleeding sluggishly. It looked up at her with pain-filled eyes as she approached, and she turned to the men above her.

'Well?' she demanded harshly. 'Aren't you going to do something?'

The men said nothing. Ellie stared at them.

'You're not going to leave it?' she demanded. 'You're vets, the three of you.'

'We have rules,' Sven said slowly. 'We are here as observers. "Take nothing but photographs. Leave nothing but footprints. And do not interfere with the natural order of things." We are here to look, Ellie, not to interfere.'

'But it'll die. . .' Ellie looked down at the seal. 'That wound has to be stitched. And it's not as if the leopard seal needs him for food.' She motioned towards the sea where the remains of the pup's companion were still discolouring the water.

Again there was silence. Ellie swore softly. 'Well, I will if you won't,' she said. She stooped to lift the seal. The seal turned and snapped, its teeth gleaming and sharp. She recoiled in dismay.

She stood up and stared helplessly down at the seal. Damn them, she thought. Heartless men! Surely they couldn't watch it slowly bleed to death? She glared up at them again, and Leeton was sliding down the rocks to join her.

She looked up as he approached, her eyes a plea. 'He can't survive with that cut,' she said softly. 'Can't we do something?'

He looked at her for a long moment and then down to the pup. Finally he spread his hands. 'OK, Dr Michaels,' he said slowly. 'Let's have a look.'

'You mean you'll help?'

'I'm breaking rules,' he said shortly. 'But if this little pup can be bitten by a leopard seal and still find the courage to try and bite you, he deserves a fighting chance.'

Ellie flushed. 'You say the nicest things,' she said tightly.

'I try.'

Leeton had stooped over the seal pup. He had thick protective gloves on, but he didn't need them. The seal was passive under his hands.

'It's only the one tear, isn't it?' Ellie asked.

'As far as I can see. I'm going to have to move him to do a complete examination.' The seal looked up at him and Leeton pursed his lips. 'A general anaesthetic, I think. . .'

'Coward,' Ellie said softly.

He grinned. 'I saw how brave you were when he snapped, Dr Michaels.' He stood. 'Over to you, then. You hold your patient's hand while I fetch what I need.'

Five minutes later the young seal was unconscious, limp in Leeton's arms and being carried up to the camp.

'I don't believe what I'm seeing,' Sven said softly as they passed. 'Rules, Lee?' He was grinning.

Leeton smiled ruefully. 'It's a seal of discernment,' he said gravely. 'Any seal who likes biting reporters. . .'

'Oh, yes,' Sven mocked. 'You mean you wouldn't have otherwise helped him.'

'I might,' Leeton retorted, without breaking stride. 'If he'd bitten you, Sven, I might also have been tempted.'

He accepted Ellie's company without comment. He walked swiftly up to the camp, laid the seal on a flat rock near their hut and started carefully swabbing the wound.

Ellie stared down at the unconscious seal. 'Do you want me to top up the anaesthetic?' she asked. Leeton shook his head.

'No. I have to work fast—wild creatures are inordinately sensitive to drugs. I'll get by on the minimum. If I have to give him more I don't like his chances.'

He was swiftly cleaning the entire area, cutting away the torn shreds of hanging skin and probing the depths of the wound.

'I'm going to have to use subcutaneous stitches,' he said shortly. 'It's deep.'

Ellie nodded. She had moved into assistant role, handing him equipment as it was required. His hands were skilled and sure. Slowly the jagged tear was pulled together.

As the subcutaneous stitches were complete, Ellie threaded Leeton's needle with the strong thread she assumed would be used for the outer layer of skin. To her surprise he shook his head and motioned to the weaker, dissolving thread.

'We haven't a patient we can bring back in ten days to remove the stitches,' he told her. 'They have to be dissolving.'

'But we'll keep him until the cut starts to heal,' Ellie said slowly. Leeton shook his head.

'We're more likely to kill him doing that than by leaving him on the beach to bleed to death.'

'Why?'

He didn't look up. His fingers were flying, expertly fitting the ragged skin together. 'Firstly we'd have to keep him confined, and after a few days he'd be stiff and lack agility in the water. Our friend the leopard seal would make short work of him. Secondly we haven't the means to provide him with the diet he's used to.'

'So you'll let him go. . .'

'As soon as he recovers from the anaesthetic,' said Leeton. 'It's his only hope.' And then, at her look of dismay, he shook his head. 'It's true, Dr Michaels,' he said. 'And if he doesn't look fit to go in a few hours then I'll put him down. It's kinder than letting him starve to death because he can't fend for himself or be ripped to death by leopard seals or orcas.'

'Orcas?'

'Killer whales.'

'Oh,' Ellie said weakly.

The tear was nearly closed. Leeton repeated his stitching over and over

'It's going to scar,' Ellie told him. 'I could do a neater job than that.'

'I'm sure you could, Dr Michaels,' he said sardonically. 'But I don't think our friend here is worried about the appearance of his wound, and by double stitching it's less likely to split open.'

She fell silent. On the rock the wounded seal began to stir. Leeton swiftly finished the last stitches, then lifted the animal into a solid crate by the hut. He closed the lid.

'A few hours of dark and quiet,' he said, 'then we assess the situation.'

'Shouldn't we be keeping him warm?' Ellie asked.

'Half an hour ago he was lying on an ice-floe,' he said. 'That box is probably the warmest place he's ever been in his life.'

'All done?' It was Sven, striding up to the huts from the beach.

'All done,' Ellie smiled at him. 'Leeton did a great job.'

Sven raised his eyebrows at his boss and his lips curved into a lazy smile. 'Well, well,' he said.

'Have you finished the banding?' Leeton asked, ignoring his friend's smile.

Sven's smile didn't slip. 'The spare boat needs patching,' he reminded Leeton. 'I think we should do it while we have some sun.' He looked at Ellie. 'Could you assist Gordon while we do this?'

'Sure,' Ellie nodded. She flicked an uncertain glance up at Leeton and then made her escape.

Gordon was still working with the petrels. He smiled up at her as she arrived and handed her a thick pair of gloves, a bag and a pile of small rings. Ellie stared down at them in dismay.

'First catch your bird,' Gordon said gently. 'It's easy.'

It wasn't easy, as she soon discovered. The men had been doing this type of work for twelve months and all were trained in veterinary science to begin with. It made a big difference.

The birds were not as docile as they looked. By the time Ellie had conquered the art of handling them, a good hour had passed and she was beginning to feel guilty at having wasted Gordon's time.

'You haven't,' he told her.

She shook her head. 'You could have managed faster without me.'

'But would we gain such a sympathetic write-up if Dr Ellie Michaels weren't personally involved?' Gordon asked honestly, and Ellie smiled.

'I know,' she said drily. 'I'm being manipulated.'

He grinned, his haggard face momentarily lighting.

'Are you looking forward to going home?' Ellie asked curiously. Sven and Leeton were taking so long that she was beginning to think it was deliberately done to give her time alone with Gordon. It seemed difficult to broach his health with him, though, when she had no right to do so.

'No.' Gordon was hanging a bird bag from the scale and jotting down the weight.

Ellie frowned. His answer had been flat and hopeless. She knew suddenly that he spoke the absolute truth.

'Why not?' she asked gently. 'Do you have family?'

'Oh, yes, I have family. As Sven told you, I have tribes of family.' He smiled, but his face was full of sadness. 'And it will be good to see them.'

'Then why don't you want to go home?'

He looked up then and met her eyes. She didn't flinch from his look. For a moment she felt he was close to some sort of breaking-point—some barrier which he sought courage to overcome. Then the bird in his grasp gave an indignant wriggle and he looked down again.

'Because I've enjoyed it here,' he said, and Ellie knew whatever was troubling him wouldn't be discussed. 'Because this is a project of international importance.'

'But you'll still be working on it at home,' she said slowly. 'I imagine the information you've collected will take years to process.'

He flashed her another look and his eyes were raw with pain. 'As you say,' he said quietly.

'Gordon, is anything wrong?' Ellie asked softly. 'You know I'm a medical doctor. Can I help you?'

His eyes went blank and expressionless. He turned back to his notes. 'No, thank you, Dr Michaels,' he said formally. 'I have no need of medical help.'

Ellie bagged another petrel neatly, becoming more proficient with each one. Her mind sought for an approach to help this man.

'Gordon, it seems to me that you might be in some sort of trouble,' she said cautiously. At his swift, repelling look she held up a gloved hand as if in denial. 'I'm not going to interfere with what's none of my business, and if whatever's worrying you and making you lose weight has been going on for months then two weeks probably won't make a difference anyway. But I'm here, and I'm available if you need help. For talk—for pain relief. . .' she smiled '. . .or just for bagging petrels and keeping my mouth shut, if that's what you'd prefer.'

He forced a weak smile and took the bird from her. 'That's what I'd prefer, Dr Michaels.'

'It's Ellie.'

He nodded and then smiled again. This time his smile reached his eyes. 'OK, Ellie. No medicine, please. It's true I have a problem, but it's one that, as you say, two weeks is going to make no difference to, and leaving now would negate much of what I've been working for. All I want from you is publicity. Just damned good publicity.'

Ellie looked at him for a long moment, reading the plea in his eyes. He was afraid she would side with Leeton—would make him leave this place before his job was done. Finally she nodded.

'Yes, sir,' she said.

Ten minutes later Leeton and Sven returned. 'All mended,' Leeton announced. He looked down to where Ellie was efficiently banding her bird. 'My, my, efficiency plus!'

'She's a fast learner,' Gordon said briefly, and his tone was a reproof.

Leeton smiled. 'I'm sorry.'

'How's the seal?' Ellie asked stiffly.

'I haven't looked,' he told her. 'He's better left undisturbed for a few hours.' He stood silently for a moment as Sven bent again to the task in hand. Finally he seemed to come to a decision.

'Could you two finish up here if I took Dr Michaels across to the rookery?' he asked Sven and Gordon. 'She should see it.'

'Sure,' Sven grinned. 'Off you go.' His grin encompassed them both, sensing Ellie's discomfort. 'See if you can make friends while you're walking. Polite chat is what Gordon and I would like over dinner, if you please.'

Ellie rose uncertainly. 'Dr Connor, I don't want to disturb your work.'

Leeton picked up her camera case. 'I'm not offering to act as tour guide because I'm trying to be nice to you,' he responded curtly.

'That's not a good start,' Sven warned.

Ellie flushed. Leeton gestured forward across the rocks, and they moved away.

'Our work here — the work of the three of us — is to find out as much as we can about man's impact on the wildlife and then let the world know,' Leeton said curtly as they moved away. 'Without you we can't do that.' He gestured towards the camera he was carrying. 'The report I received said you were a decent photographer. Wildlife or chocolate-box kittens?'

Ellie was walking at an almost stumbling run trying to keep up with the man beside her. They were making their way across the rocks, around the first headland of the island. She looked up at Leeton and then back down to the rocks she was negotiating.

'The magazine put me through an intensive photography course,' she said through gritted teeth. 'If you want me to photograph wildlife then that's what I'll

photograph. If, however, I need to photograph kittens——' She broke off, her anger threatening to choke
her.

Silence stretched out between them. They were
around the headland and into the next cove before it
was broken. Finally Leeton gave a short, harsh laugh.

'Well, whatever you are, I guess I'm just stuck with
it,' he said grimly. 'I just hope against faint hope that
you know the job you're here for.'

Ellie walked and fumed. She was struggling to catch
up, but she would rather die than admit she was having
difficulties. Despite what he had done for her seal, this
man was an arrogant toad. She thought back to the
article she had written for the *Daily* and shook her head.
It had been too mild, she thought savagely. This man
deserved everything she had written about him and
more.

'Did you talk to Gordon?' he asked suddenly.

Ellie considered before answering. She would have
liked to tell Dr Connor that Gordon's health was none
of his business, but the temptation was stupid. Leeton
was in charge of this small group, and he was rightly
concerned.

'I tried,' she said stiffly. 'He doesn't want to talk.'

'Are you worried?'

Ellie stared at her feet, willing them to move faster as
she considered the question. 'Yes,' she said finally.
'There is something wrong. And the man's afraid.' She
thought for a moment. 'Why not send him over to
Kellent for a complete examination? If you're in charge
he has to go if you ordered it.'

Leeton shook his head. 'I won't do that to him,' he
said. There was silence for a moment as though he was
considering his options. 'Stephen Ryde is medical officer
for the entire area,' he said finally. 'What he says goes.
He knows I'm worried and he knows how isolated this
place is. Even if he can't find anything specific wrong,

he's not going to let Gordon come back here. Would you?'

Ellie turned this over. 'No,' she said finally. 'If I had to make that decision I couldn't be responsible for allowing him to return. Not the way he looks.'

Leeton nodded. 'And Gordon's work here is as important to him as mine is to me. If I thought I'd be saving his life by sending him to Kellent then I would. But you don't think that's likely.'

'He might have cancer,' Ellie said slowly.

'And if it's making him sick enough to look the way he does, is a fortnight going to make such a difference?'

'It might.' She considered. 'Gordon admits that there's something wrong, though, and he assures me two weeks won't make a difference.'

'And Gordon's not a fool,' Leeton said slowly, as if trying to make a decision. 'He's a vet, for heaven's sake. He'll know the chances. I was worried about stomach ulcers or leukaemia.'

'Both are improbable,' Ellie told him, 'not impossible.'

'And stress is still an option?'

'Improbable again,' she said shortly.

'OK.' Leeton took a deep breath. 'Well, we have our own doctor on hand, albeit a dubious one. I think that's all I can do.'

Ellie said nothing.

It was almost an hour of solid walking before they negotiated a rocky outcrop and found what they had set out to find. The rocks were teeming with penguins — groups of three-quarter-grown adelies. They were grey, rather than the stark black and white of the parent birds, still fluffy with their baby down and all intent on one thing — the arrival of the parent birds with the means to satisfy, at least momentarily, their insatiable hunger.

The noise was amazing, but the overwhelming sensation was the stench. The ground was covered with layer upon layer of guano — penguin excrement.

'It decomposes very slowly,' Leeton said ruefully. 'At this time of year it defrosts for a few hours at a time, stinks, then refreezes with smell intact.'

Ellie didn't care. She was moving among the chicks with care.

It was a photographer's paradise. The place was one of unbridled beauty — where landscape and penguin combined in a picture that had remained unchanged for thousands of years.

'Millions,' Ellie said exultantly. 'It's. . . I feel that I haven't any right here.'

Leeton was watching her thoughtfully. He nodded. 'It's not our place,' he said definitely. 'But we are changing it.' He motioned towards a limp form some few yards from them. Striding over, he stooped to examine a dead penguin. The body was that of a full-grown female. Beside it was that of a chick.

'The chick's just dead,' Leeton said briefly, 'otherwise the skuas would have disposed of it. The mother's been dead for a day or so.'

'I guess there have to be deaths in a colony as big as this,' Ellie said slowly. She crossed to stoop beside him. Leeton's fingers were probing, peforming a careful examination of the mother's semi-frozen remains.

'The death-rate of chicks is almost forty per cent,' he told her. 'This is the harshest environment in the world to try to raise young. They have enough hazards to face without the ones we add, though. This death is down to us.'

Ellie's hooded face creased into a frown as she stared down at the pathetic pair. 'Why?'

Leeton sighed. 'Antarctica may have been unchanged for thousands of years, but it's changing now.' He ran his finger lightly through the bird's thick coat then put his finger to his nose. 'Diesel oil,' he said briefly. 'One of the boats has had a spill. The oil will have damaged the waterproofing on the feathers and she'll have died of cold. Chicks need two parents to rear them successfully. It will have starved to death. Somewhere out there will be the male, disorientated and deprived of both mate and young.'

Ellie was silent. The death seemed almost sacrilegious in this place of wonder. Finally she raised her camera. Angling the lens until she caught the sheen of oil on the bird's coat, she photographed until she was sure she had the shot she wanted — the pathetic death of mother and chick. It wasn't the beautiful side of her story on Antarctica, but it was one that would have to be presented.

Finally she stood and looked round. 'I can't see any more dead adult birds,' she said dubiously.

'No.' Leeton shrugged. 'A tiny spill, perhaps covering only a square foot of water surface, will do this. While any human settlement is here this type of thing will happen.' He ran a hand wearily through his hair. 'But they're talking of drilling for oil down here. Imagine that, Ellie. Imagine the potential for absolute disaster.'

'Surely it won't happen,' she said doubtfully. 'Surely people can see there have to be places left untouched. . .'

He shrugged. 'It's up to you,' he said briefly. 'There's plans for an airfield at the moment, straight across the breeding path of the emperor penguins. The penguins will find another path, we're told. But the research we're doing suggests that the penguins have been following the same paths throughout time, and disorientated birds die. The only answer — to either resite the airstrip or not build it at all — is totally unacceptable.' He smiled grimly. 'They might just find they have a fight on their hands.'

Ellie nodded. 'We'll help,' she said simply. It was just

the sort of cause *Our Planet's Health* was designed to publicise.

Leeton shook his head. 'The people who read *Our Planet's Health* are already converted,' he told her. 'We need massive publicity.'

Ellie frowned at the man beside her. 'You can get that,' she said slowly, 'because of who you are. . .'

'The first rule of publicity-seeking,' Leeton said drily. 'First make yourself notorious. . . Maybe you can convince yourself you've done me a favour, Dr Michaels.' He shrugged. 'You'd better get yourself some shots of the whole colony.' He turned away and left her to it.

Ellie stood for a moment, her cheeks burning. Damn that article, she thought. He would never put it from his mind. She put her hands to her face and fought for calm.

She couldn't keep thinking about it. What was done was done, and Leeton's cold disdain was something she would have to live with.

There was only one thing that could matter now. She, Ellie Michaels, was in the middle of a photographer's paradise, and her time was limited. There was no time now for regrets. She raised her camera and started work.

An hour later she surfaced, almost satisfied. What Leeton had been doing she had no idea. Looking up from the chick she had just photographed, she thought for a moment that he had left her. Shading her eyes from the glare, she finally found him, sitting on a rock surveying her with lazy ease. She swung her camera back up to her eye and took a couple of shots of the man, seated with such casual ease in this desolate setting. Even in his many layers of clothing there was no disguising his rugged good looks. As he realised what she was doing he raised his hand in a negative gesture, rose and came towards her.

'Finished?' he asked.

She shook her head. 'I could stay here for the next two weeks and not be finished. My film isn't inexhaustible, though.'

He smiled at her, his heart-stopping smile that made her insides do strange things. Obviously she had done right for a change, she thought bitterly.

'You must be hungry,' he said.

'No.' She looked up at him uncertainly and then considered. 'Well, maybe. . .'

He smiled again, reached into a back-pack and produced some sandwiches. 'Lunch.' He glanced at his watch. 'Even if it is a couple of hours late. I was going to suggest we eat as soon as we arrived, but I was distracted.'

Ellie picked up her equipment and came over to him.

'Great,' she said dubiously.

'What's the matter?'

For answer she held up a hand to her nose and wrinkled her nose in distaste. This place had been a penguin rookery for generations, and it seemed that the guano from every penguin that had ever lived here was still as strong-smelling as the day it had been deposited.

Leeton laughed unsympathetically. 'How hungry are you?' he grinned.

Ellie considered. Suddenly breakfast seemed a long way away. She peeled off her outer gloves, took a deep breath and tackled a sandwich.

'Where on earth did you get bread?' she asked curiously.

'They make it at Kellent,' Leeton said briefly. 'We had new supplies yesterday, and freezing isn't exactly a problem. A bigger problem is thawing, but they've been against my back for a couple of hours. The body warmth has done the trick.'

They ate silently. The wind had faded to non-existence. Around them, fat chicks waddled awkwardly. Out to sea, the water was alive with the parent birds, surfacing for the last stretch of water, then shooting out to land in a glistening heap on the rocks. The sea was calm and still, with floes of crystal-like ice dotting the surface. The sun was almost warm on Ellie's face.

The smell was forgotten. She leaned back on her rock and gazed entranced at the view in front of her. It was an untouched Eden.

Out to sea the surface of the water was suddenly broken. Slabs of ice were thrust upward as a huge black form broke the surface. Beside it was another, much smaller. A whale and her calf. . .

Ellie's last sandwich fell to the ground unheeded as she reached frantically for her camera. The whale and her calf obliged. They breached again and again, giving her time to adjust her lenses and take all the shots she wanted. Their huge, blue-black bodies gleamed in the weak sunlight. Again and again the tails broke the surface, one massive and the other a miniature copy, throwing up clouds of spray. It was as if the mother was showing off her baby to the world. Look at us, her actions were proclaiming. We are magnificent.

Finally the show was over. The whales sank out of sight for the last time. Ellie took a deep breath and relaxed.

'Wasn't that. . .?' She shook her head. Words couldn't describe how she was feeling. She turned to Leeton and found him watching her. The expression on his face was of absolute confusion.

For a moment she met his eyes. The old tension resurfaced between them, and Ellie felt her confusion mirrored in his eyes. What was happening between them? She didn't understand. She didn't want to understand.

She bent to retrieve the remnants of her sandwich, now fouled by the all-pervasive penguin guano. The time it took to dispose of the scrap with the other remains of their lunch gave her time to regain her composure.

'Not a litter-bug, Ellie?' It was an attempt at light humour, and she recognised it as an unsure attempt to mask the emotional charge running between them. She looked up at him quickly, then, as quickly, away again.

'No one's been this way for thousands of years, by the look of this place,' she responded, trying to follow his lead. 'I don't want the next person here to recognise the remains of Ellie Michaels' lunch.' She slung her camera bag over her shoulder. 'Shall we go?'

Leeton smiled and started walking. Beside him she tried to maintain his pace while her head spun. His smile, lighting up his face and turning his forbidding features into a concerned and caring human being, suddenly made her aware of what she had been hiding from herself for the last two years.

When Sam had walked out of their marriage she had sworn that no man would touch her again; that no man would affect her life. This man beside her didn't even have to touch her to affect her. Her body was alight with the awareness of his presence. This man. . .

This man was danger, to the carefully built up armour she had created around her heart. A young and foolish Ellie Michaels could have become another of Leeton Connor's conquests, she told herself harshly. One look from him and her body responded with an arousal that no man had ever created in her. Now. . .

Somehow the armour had to be strengthened. Somehow her defences had to be maintained until in two weeks she could leave this place and never see Leeton Connor again.

CHAPTER FIVE

Sven and Gordon were still at work down at the nesting grounds when they reached camp. From the crate beside the hut came the sounds of an animal being kept against its will.

'It seems our patient's awake,' Leeton said. 'Do you want to look?'

Ellie nodded slowly and walked over to the crate. Carefully she lifted the lid, allowing the light to penetrate the crate. From inside the box a ball of grey fury launched itself at her, hissing and spitting. It couldn't climb the steep sides, but its anger was enough to make her drop the lid and take a step back. Leeton laughed unsympathetically.

'It seems he's healthy,' he smiled. 'If he hadn't reacted like that, I'd have had to put him down. But he seems fine.' He lifted the lid again and inspected the pup, still spitting its indignation.

'OK, Dr Michaels, we have a job to do.'

'What?' Ellie asked curiously.

'We need to carry him around the headland and release him. And I'm not carrying him in my arms while he's awake.'

'Why don't we let him out here?' she said in dismay. The crate looked heavy. 'He could get to the water himself.'

'To the cove, yes,' Leeton said drily. 'But the cove is the leopard seal's domain, and I don't want our pup trying himself out in the water with the leopard seal watching.' He picked up a handle of the crate. 'Ready?'

Ellie took a deep breath and nodded. 'Ready.'

It was harder than she thought, and Leeton didn't

spare her. It was as if he was deliberately testing her, she thought grimly, struggling to heave the crate over the rocks. Finally, though, they rounded the headland, and took the crate down to the water's edge. Leeton flipped up the top and tipped the crate, the seal gave one last angry hiss and disappeared into the water.

'You'd think he could have said thank you,' Ellie smiled. 'Ungrateful beast.'

'If he'd come to trust us we couldn't have released him,' Leeton said firmly.

'Do you think he'll survive?'

'He might.'

'Only might. . .'

'He has a chance,' Leeton said, relenting slightly. 'We've given him that. And that's all we can do.'

There was nothing more to be said. Ellie looked up at him, but he was staring out to sea, watching the ripples settle after the pup's hurried splash. She turned away and picked up her handle of the empty crate. It was impossible to tell what this man was thinking.

Back at the hut Leeton hesitated as Ellie turned to go inside.

'We need to get the banding completed tonight,' he told her. 'Will you help?'

She shook her head. Her exposed films were accumulating. She hadn't been able to develop any on the ship, and she was anxious to know if her allowance for the harsh Antarctic light was correct.

'You go,' she told Leeton. 'I need a couple of hours in the hut by myself.'

'Exhausted already?' His tone was sardonic.

She flushed. 'No. I want to use the hut as a darkroom.' She forced herself to smile sweetly. 'I'm afraid for the next two hours you'll be forced to find alternative accommodation.'

It was more than two hours before she had the results she wanted. Covering the hut windows to block the light was difficult, and she was almost tempted to ask for Leeton's help. Almost. She struggled on by herself until she finally had it to her satisfaction.

Her results were worth the effort. One by one the photographs emerged, and Ellie's tension eased as she realised how good they were.

The photographs of the dead penguin with its chick brought a lump to her throat, and she knew it would find a prominent place in *Our Planet's Health* — it was a tragic example of the consequence of thoughtlessness. She produced it first then went on to the shots whose sole purpose was to show the absolute magnificence of this continent.

There were seals floating lazily on the ice, penguins half submerged in the glistening water, the white flash of the snow petrels against the black Antarctic sea and the massive body of the whales, breaching through the ice. Time was forgotten as Ellie produced one wonderful photograph after another.

Finally she printed the last shots, the shots of Leeton. Here were photographs that would sell copies of *Our Planet's Health* to people who had never heard of the magazine.

It was Leeton Connor as Americans had never seen him, lounging against the barren rocks of the Antarctic. Behind him were jagged ridges of ice and around him was a sea of penguin chicks. The hood of his anorak was swept back, his dark hair was wind-swept, and his eyes were creased against the glare. His hands were deep in the pockets of his jacket as he looked out over the icy terrain. Here was a man at ease; at peace with his environment.

Ellie stared down at the expression, the half-smile on Leeton's face, taken as he had looked across at her, and felt her heart knot in confusion. This was the man she had described to Americans as being 'totally dependent on the trappings of his wealth'.

There was a knock on the metal door and she pulled her gaze away from the photographs and looked at her watch. With a shock she realised it was almost nine p.m.

'Finished?' It was Leeton.

She shoved the shots of Leeton out of sight. The others he could see, but these were not for his eyes. Finally she opened the door of the hut, allowing the weak light to penetrate. Leeton was standing with a plate of steaming meat casserole in his hand.

'Your dinner, ma'am.'

'Thank you.' She took the plate gratefully. 'There was no need to bring it over — I've finished.'

'So have we.' He looked pointedly at his watch. 'We ate an hour ago. If we kept this hot much longer it'd resemble our more inedible dehydrated rations.' His eyes were on the photographs behind her. 'May I see?'

'Mmm.' Ellie moved in and sat on the remaining bunk. She had folded Leeton's out of the way to give her more room while she worked. She sat and ate as he slowly worked his way through her photographs.

She found she was almost holding her breath waiting for his comments. She knew her work was good, but this man would be her harshest critic. She watched as, without expression, he picked up one photograph after another. Finally he laid the last one down and turned to where she was trying to concentrate on her casserole.

'They're magnificent,' he told her.

Ellie nodded. 'I'm happy with them,' she said simply. She didn't look up.

There was a long-drawn-out silence in the little hut. Leeton was staring at her as if he was seeing her for the first time and couldn't believe what he was seeing.

'With a talent like this, what the hell were you doing working for a sensationalist, muck-racking rag like the *Daily*?' he demanded.

Ellie finished the food on her plate then looked up to meet his baffled expression.

'That's none of your business,' she said quietly.

He looked at her, considering. 'I suppose it was the money,' he said at last.

She bit her lip, trying to maintain her calm. 'That's right,' she said equably. 'I'm out for what I can get. That's why I moved to *Our Planet's Health*. The money's fantastic.'

'I know exactly how much you earn.'

She nodded. 'I guessed you'd have found that out,' she said wearily. 'With your contacts you could even find out which brand of underwear I buy.'

As soon as she had said the words she knew she had made a grave mistake. His look deepened into a grin, the harshness disappearing from his expression.

'With my contacts? I don't think I need my contacts to find that out.'

Ellie stood up abruptly, her eyes flashing anger. 'If you'll excuse me, Dr Connor, I need to say goodnight to Sven and Gordon.'

He laid a hand placatingly on her shoulder. 'I'm sorry.' The smile was still there, lurking behind the grey of his eyes. Ellie gasped as the smile intensified. 'Don't worry,' he told her, 'the brand of your underwear can remain your own personal secret.' Then, disregarding the rising anger in her eyes, he gathered the dry photographs together.

'Come on, Ellie Michaels of the unknown underwear,' he grinned. 'Sven has coffee on, and both he and Gordon will be delighted with these. Gordon's cut his hand, by the way. I'd like you to have a look at it.'

Sven was standing beside the little stove as they entered the other hut. Ellie carried her medical bag in and put it down. Gordon was wrapping his hand in a thick wad of bandage. From where she stood, Ellie could make out the faint tinge of blood seeping through. He looked over to the medical bag and frowned.

'I don't need that.'

Ellie smiled and walked over to him. 'Dr Connor told me you'd hurt it. He's shown off his needlework. I thought I might be able to show off mine.'

'It does need stitching,' Sven said briefly.

To her surprise Gordon snatched his hand back, cradling it protectively with the other.

'It's nothing,' he said brusquely.

'How did it happen?'

'He was bitten by a skua,' Sven said quietly, casting a worried look at Gordon. 'We'd just weighed a petrel and she had a chick in her nest. The skua thought he'd help himself to the chick. Gordon objected to the skua and the skua objected to Gordon.' He shrugged. 'With skuas you need special protective gloves, which Gordon wasn't wearing.'

'Can I see?' Ellie asked Gordon.

'I've cleaned it and put antiseptic on,' he told her. 'Nothing more needs to be done.'

'I wish you'd let Dr Michaels look at it.' Leeton was watching Gordon through narrowed eyes. 'Sven says it's jagged and deep.'

'How would he know?' Gordon snapped.

Sven shrugged. 'It's true,' he told Ellie. 'I wasn't permitted to help. But what I saw concerned me.'

'Oh, for heaven's sake. . .' Gordon's voice was both weary and angry. 'I've done everything that needs to be done, and I'm damned if I'm unwrapping it just for "show and tell".' He managed a half-smile then turned to Sven. 'The only attention I need is a cup of coffee.'

There was silence in the hut. Ellie half expected Leeton to come out with a direct order for the hand to be unwrapped. It didn't come.

'I'd like some coffee too,' he said finally, crossing to sit beside Gordon on the bunk. 'And look what our Dr

Michaels has come up with. She might just deserve a cup too.'

The gathering relaxed. The photographs released the tension in a way nothing else could, and Ellie could tell by the sudden shift in conversation and the thoughtful expressions on the men's faces that her usefulness was being reappraised.

Gordon spent a long time looking at Ellie's close-up shots of ice formations, then turned to her, his hand forgotten in his enthusiasm.

'You could photograph my algae.'

Ellie choked on her coffee and all the men laughed.

'You've been singularly honoured, Ellie,' Leeton explained, and for the first time she noted the transition to her first name. 'It looks as if you're going to be permitted to photograph Gordon's skuas and his algae. They're equally attractive, I'd say.' He grimaced expressively and was punched firmly by Gordon's good hand. 'Though perhaps Gordon's gone off skuas,' he smiled.

'I asked for what I got,' Gordon said firmly. 'I left a chick defenceless and then I interfered again in the natural order of things in preventing the skua from taking it.' He grinned at Leeton. 'Sometimes your rules do apply.'

Leeton nodded. 'Interfere with this environment and accept the consequences,' he said lightly. He hesitated. 'Photography of the algae would be useful if you could do it,' he said slowly. 'A lot of our work is centred on algae.'

'Why?' asked Ellie.

'Algae grows on the underside of the ice here,' Leeton explained. 'In summer, as the ice melts, the algae are released into the water to provide a major food source for the krill. The krill are tiny, shrimplike creatures that are the food of just about every other form of life here. We're trying to establish how the gradual warming of the earth's temperature could affect the growth and release of algae and hence the krill, and thus the rest of the wildlife here. Some great photography might just get us government interest. It's a little hard arousing public sympathy for algae.'

Ellie's mind was whirling in amazement. Her prejudices were being torn apart. Was this the same man who had shown her through his stable of thoroughbred horses? Who had shown her through one of his three magnificent homes? Who had been photographed with one society beauty after another? Could that memory of Leeton from two years before be the same man who was now pleading the cause of *algae*?

'Well?' Gordon was saying anxiously.

'I. . . I don't know.' Ellie was still dumbfounded. 'It would be close-up work. . . I guess I could do it.' She looked up at Leeton. 'I've taken shots of microsurgery for the magazine. It shouldn't be too different.'

'Except you'll be in a rocking boat in freezing conditions while you do it,' Leeton grinned. 'But you're right, it shouldn't be too different.'

'Well?' Gordon demanded again. 'If it's calm I want to collect samples from the cove tomorrow. Will you come in the boat and photograph them as they come from the water? They're not as good by the time I get them back to the shore,' he explained.

'I'd be delighted,' Ellie agreed, her puzzled eyes still on Leeton.

'Have you finished your coffee?' He met her gaze squarely.

'I. . . Yes. . .'

He held out a hand and pulled her to her feet. 'Then I think, Dr Michaels, that it's time we said goodnight. It's well after midnight. If you're not exhausted, I am.'

'You mean you're sending me to bed?' She attempted a smile, but it didn't quite come off.

'Oh, I'm coming too,' he said calmly. He put up a

hand to acknowledge Sven and Gordon. 'Goodnight, gentlemen. Dr Michaels and I have some serious sleeping to do.'

'Why the hell wouldn't he let you see his hand?' Leeton exploded as soon as the door was shut behind them. With the hum of the wind in the steel cables they were safely out of Gordon's hearing.

'Perhaps he doesn't like doctors,' Ellie said lightly, and Leeton shook his head.

'The man's a vet himself, for heaven's sake! From what I saw, that cut needs stitching, but to get it stitched I'm going to have to issue a direct order.'

Ellie turned to face him. 'Why don't you?' she asked simply.

He stared at her for a long moment and she knew he was not seeing her. 'I'm nominally in charge of this expedition, but we're a team,' he said slowly. 'Both Gordon and Sven are experts in their own fields, and I'm damned if I'll insult their independence unless it's absolutely essential. Gordon's old enough not to need a nursemaid. He won't risk infection, and the fact that it'll scar without stitching is not my concern.'

Ellie nodded.

'I'm starting to think the whole thing—his weight loss—everything—is stress-related,' Leeton went on, as though reassuring himself. 'His behaviour with his hand was crazy. If we had six months ahead of us I'd be insisting he see a doctor for a complete check, but I guess with only a fortnight to go I can leave him be.'

Once again Ellie nodded, but not because she was agreeing with him. A seed of suspicion had planted itself in her mind and she was turning a tentative diagnosis over and over.

If she was right then Leeton could just as well go on believing Gordon's problems were stress-related, because a fortnight should make little difference. But Ellie didn't like what her mind was starting to tell her.

Whether or not Ellie needed to do some 'serious sleeping', the sleep was a long time coming. Once ensconced in the warmth of her bag she lay in the fading light and willed herself to ignore the man in the hut with her.

Leeton was longer than Ellie in reaching his bed. He methodically filled out a journal before shedding his clothes. She turned to the wall as he had done for her.

'Safe now.' She felt her bunk shift slightly as Leeton climbed into his. 'You can look.'

'Goodnight,' she said stiffly.

'I wouldn't close your eyes quite yet,' he said softly.

'Why not?' Her voice was strained.

'You'd miss this.' He leaned forward and pulled her shoulders into sitting position, then turned her resisting head to the porthole.

Ellie opened her eyes reluctantly, then gasped and opened them wider. An hour before, when she had entered the hut, the sun had been close to setting. Now it was a sliver of fiery orange on the horizon across the bay, sending shards of brilliant crimson and yellow across the sky to light the snow-laden clouds. Below, the sea was on fire with reflected colour, and beyond was the deep black ridge of the Antarctic mainland.

The cold and Leeton's presence was forgotten. Ellie stared, entranced. Finally the compulsion was too great. Ignoring Leeton, she climbed out of her bag to fetch her camera.

Leeton's bunk was between her and her equipment and she was forced to negotiate his inert body. He lay back, his arms behind his head, and watched her with amusement.

'Am I in your way?' he asked politely.

Ellie's face broke into a grin. She searched for and found the equipment she needed, then clambered back again on to her bunk. 'Not at all,' she answered with equal civility. Then he was ignored until she had captured the scene from her porthole to her satisfaction.

Finally the magnificent display was over. The last wisps of crimson faded and she turned from the glass with regret.

Leeton smiled. 'Worth the trip?' he prodded.

She smiled. 'And then some.' She looked down at the cameras in her hands then over to the bags on the other side of Leeton.

'Don't mind me,' he said resignedly. 'I'm used to being treated as a doormat.'

'So I've noticed,' Ellie said drily, but took him at his word. He lay back and suffered in silence while she negotiated his bunk. Finally she crawled back into her bag and lay there, shivering. She hadn't been dressed for sitting up in the cold taking photographs.

'Cold?'

'No.' Ellie pulled her bag up under her chin and clenched her teeth.

'I can think of an efficient method of warming you,' Leeton said helpfully.

'I'm sure you can,' she said between chattering teeth. 'Thank you, but I can do without it.'

There was silence between them. It was almost dark. Ellie stared into the gloom and concentrated on sleep. She was rigidly aware of Leeton's body.

'Still cold?'

'No.' It was a lie.

Silence again.

There was no way she could block out Leeton's presence. The sound of his quiet breathing was enough to keep her tense and awake. In a warmer climate she would have taken her bag outside and slept under the stars rather than go through this.

Here there was no choice. She could even sleep better crammed into the other hut between Sven and Gordon, she thought, then questioned herself angrily as to why. Sven and Gordon were men too. Why didn't her body react to them in the same way?

'Tell me why you're here,' she said harshly, breaking the stillness. Her voice echoed oddly in the confined space.

'Me?' Leeton stirred.

'Who else do you think I'd be talking to?' Her tone was brusque and abrupt, but she didn't care.

'I beg your pardon?' His voice was gravely courteous. 'I believe I was asleep.'

'Well, I'm not.' Ellie turned over to face the dark shadow beside her. 'My instructions are not to waste a minute.'

'So you'd like an in-depth interview at midnight.' He sighed and rolled over to look at her. 'I'm here because the Antarctic continent and its wildlife has been an enduring interest of mine since I was a teenager,' he said quietly. 'I'm here because my aim since then has been to help in any way I can to preserve the species of this magnificent continent.'

Ellie thought back to the man she had interviewed two years ago. 'I don't believe you,' she said flatly.

'That's your prerogative.' His voice was unperturbed. 'After all, a man who, according to your article, has lived for nothing but pleasure, is attached to no one and is incapable of attachment to anything but his wealth, must surely expect not to be believed. Now you'll excuse me. Unlike you, Dr Michaels, I need my sleep.'

He turned away, his breathing already deepening. Ellie was left to stare at the shifting patterns on the rounded ceiling before exhaustion finally closed her eyes.

She woke early, far earlier than the day could begin. She glanced at her watch. It was five a.m. She knew she had no chance of drifting back to sleep. Beside her, Leeton's breathing was deep and even.

She lay on her back and stared at the metal roof of the hut. She felt strange, drifting, as if someone else rather than Ellie Michaels were in her body. So much had happened to her in the last few days. The Ellie Michaels of New York seemed like a stranger.

Finally she could bear the stillness no longer. She pushed the sleeping-bag away, pulling her thick sweater on as she did. She was learning fast. Thoughtful dressing was something she did in New York. In the Antarctic she dressed for speed.

There wasn't a lot of trouble she could go to anyway. The huge sexless trousers and sweaters she had been supplied with were designed for comfort and practicality. Designer fashions had not yet made their appearance in the Antarctic.

Beside her Leeton slept on. Finally clothed, Ellie slid carefully over the base of his bunk, trying not to disturb him. As she reached the tiny floor space he stirred.

'Going somewhere?'

'For a walk,' she said shortly. 'I can't sleep.'

'Guilty conscience,' he said definitely, his voice slurred with sleep.

'If that stopped people sleeping you'd never close your eyes,' she retorted.

He smiled. 'Well, Ellie Michaels, I'll have you know my conscience is perfectly clear. Do you want company on this walk?'

'No.'

'Just as well,' he said in a muffled tone as he buried his face further down into his hood. 'I don't think Gordon or Sven would wish to be woken.'

Despite the tension of the night before, Ellie smiled.

'What time will you be back?' Leeton queried from the depths of his bag.

'I don't know.'

'Make a time and stick to it,' he said firmly. 'And tell me where you're going.'

'Yes, sir.'

'It's an absolute rule, Ellie. Eight o'clock?'

'OK.'

'And where?'

'I. . . I don't know. I intend to leave the hut and turn left.'

'That'll do,' he said drowsily. 'It's a small island. Leave yourself more time to come back than you take going. It always takes longer, and the wind rises as the day advances.'

'Yes, sir.'

'And don't go close to the water on your own.'

'No, sir.' It was all she could do not to salute. She left the hut and closed the door, being careful to avoid the usual harsh clang of the metal door.

Outside the wind was brisk, but bearable. Ellie made a quick trip to the 'bathroom', then emerged to face the day.

For a moment she thought she had the world to herself. The island was bleak and barren in the harsh dawn light. Then, as she took stock of the day, she saw a lone figure sitting on a rock down near the shoreline. Gordon.

If anyone needed his sleep it was Gordon. For a moment Ellie hesitated, reluctant to intrude on what was obviously a silent vigil. The man was perfectly still, his face turned into the wind. Then, as the solitude of the lone man caught at her, she knew she had to try again to approach him. She walked slowly down to join him.

'Is this Insomniacs Anonymous?' she asked softly. 'Can I join in?'

He turned, his face changing, but not quickly enough for her to miss the utter bleakness that had been there before.

He moved over, allowing room on his rock for her to be seated beside him. 'Be my guest.'

Ellie sat. For a while she didn't say anything, just sat staring out at the slate-grey and white of the heaving sea and ice.

'It's magnificent, isn't it?' she said quietly, finally. Gordon nodded. 'Is your hand hurting?'

'No.'

'I'd like to be allowed to help.'

He shook his head. 'You can't,' he said bleakly.

Ellie took a deep breath. Turning towards him, she took his gloved hands into hers.

'Gordon, I'm guessing what's wrong. And I'm telling you that I'm here and I'd very much like to help. I'm a doctor.' She sighed. 'And I could also be a friend if you let me. I have a feeling you could do with one.'

He pulled back, staring at her with expressionless eyes.

'You've guessed. . .'

'I don't know anything unless you tell me,' Ellie reassured him.

'You mean. . .you won't tell Lee?'

'I can't tell him what I haven't been told,' she said firmly. Her hands caught his again. 'There's no weakness in accepting help, though, Gordon. Lee and Sven are your friends, much more so than I am. They're concerned, and you'd find them totally supportive, I know.' As Ellie said the words she marvelled at her surety that she was telling the truth. Two years ago she wouldn't have made such a statement about Leeton Connor.

Gordon was shaking his head. 'There's two weeks to go,' he said heavily, 'and then I can go home and face what I have to face back there. Not here. This is my last Eden, Ellie.' He stared out over the water and his voice broke. 'My last Eden,' he said softly.

Ellie left him there. The man was lost in his own

thoughts; his own unhappiness. She ached for him, but knew that he needed to be alone. It was all she could do for him.

She left the cove and set off in the opposite direction to the penguin colony she and Leeton had seen the day before, treading carefully over the slippery, ice-covered rocks. Her soft rubber boots gripped firmly, but care was still required. She wasn't crazy about the idea of being immobilised with a sprained ankle for the rest of her stay.

On impulse she turned slightly inland, starting to climb the ridge behind the camp. The rocky terrain rose sharply and soon she was out of breath. Still she climbed.

The thought of Gordon went over and over in her mind. What on earth could she do? Nothing, she decided. She couldn't even talk to Leeton. Gordon had made it perfectly clear he wanted nothing made public. And besides, her diagnosis was still supposition.

Her physical exertion gradually drove Gordon to the back of her mind. Her attention had to be totally on finding footholds on the slippery rock.

At one point she paused in amazement. Above her head was a waterfall, frozen in perpetual motion. Later in the day as the sun gained strength it would flow again, fed by the melting ice above, only to re-freeze as the temperature dropped that night.

Her camera, never far away, was brought into action. For the first time Ellie began to be concerned as to whether she really had brought enough film. Everywhere there were photographs just begging to be taken. Reluctantly she tore her gaze away from the frozen cascade and started to climb again.

Finally the rise petered out to a rocky plateau. Here was flat, barren, rock-strewn terrain, interspersed with vast rounded boulders, polished by thousands of years of lying under a moving ice-cap, and shining in the weak morning light.

Ellie walked to the highest boulder and climbed, using her soft rubber boots to gain a grip on the slippery surface.

She might have been the only inhabitant of the world. Around her were rocks, ice, and further away, in a broad sweep around the island, the slate-grey of the sea. There was nothing else. Above her head a snow petrel flashed past, its pure white slashing the sky. The sunlight caught its whiteness, making her gasp with its beauty. She raised her camera, then lowered it. How could she capture such beauty?

She sat and let her surroundings take effect. They soaked into her, soothing her weary mind. So much had happened. So much was happening.

She let her mind drift back to the past, to Sam. He had walked out on her, leaving her with her trust shattered, her precarious pride in tatters. One day she had thought theirs was a stable marriage and the next it was finished. She had sacrificed so much for nothing. It was no wonder she had reacted with such violence.

The article she had written on Leeton Connor had been the most vitriolic of her career. She was beginning to admit that it not only hadn't been deserved but that her innuendoes were crass untruths. It had just been unfortunate that Leeton Connor had been in the way of her hurt and her anger.

In the way. . . She turned the phrase over in her mind. Leeton Connor was still very much 'in the way'. No matter how she twisted, her mind always returned to his enigmatic look; his lean, muscled body.

She shook herself angrily. She didn't trust Leeton Connor. She had trusted Sam and he had betrayed her trust completely. Who else could she trust?

The answer was no one. She could no longer even

trust herself. When she was near Leeton Connor her body betrayed her.

She sat on the broad rock-face, letting the weak sun do its best to warm her and listening to the stirring of the wind through the bare hills. She felt an overwhelming urge to stay exactly where she was; to never move again. It was all just too hard. She closed her eyes and leaned back against her rock.

CHAPTER SIX

'WHAT the hell do you think you're playing at?'

Ellie jerked into wakefulness. The rock was hard beneath her, the sun was warm on her face and Leeton was standing directly above her, his eyes angry and accusing.

'What. . .?' She struggled into a sitting position, shaking off sleep. 'I must have dozed off.'

'Obviously.' Leeton's voice was grim. He held out his watch. 'Nine o'clock, Dr Michaels. You gave me a return time of eight.'

Ellie bit her lip. 'You needn't have worried,' she said quietly. 'I'm fine.'

'So I can see.' He was standing over her, his posture and expression forbidding. 'Unfortunately we follow rules in this camp. No matter how much we'd like a member of the party to break her silly little neck, if she gives us a return time of eight and is an hour late, it's part of the rules that we look for her.'

Ellie got stiffly to her feet. Leeton made no move to assist her.

'I'm sorry,' she said, tilting her head defiantly. 'I'd hate to think I put you to any trouble.'

He laughed. 'I'll bet you would.'

'There's no need to be sarcastic. I said I was sorry.'

'It seems to be a habit of yours,' he said sardonically. 'The Ellie Michaels Code: do what you like and say sorry to make it right again.'

Ellie slid down the boulder. She could make no answer to his accusations.

'Are Gordon and Sven looking too?' she asked guiltily.

He shook his head. He didn't drop to join her, but

stayed on the boulder, gazing at the bleak landscape spread before him. When he spoke Ellie knew his thoughts were only partly on her.

'No. I thought it'd be a fool's errand. Gordon watched you come up this way, and we assumed you'd forgotten the time.' He hesitated, then said softly, almost to himself, 'It's easy enough to do in this place.'

'You've been up here before?' Ellie asked curiously, her resentment put aside for the moment.

'It's the hightest point. I've spent some time here.'

'Just looking?' She was trying to come to terms with the man she thought she knew, as opposed to this cold-eyed stranger, standing along on the rock, looking not at her but at the vast, bleak continent surrounding him.

'Just looking.' He turned reluctantly and stepped down to join her. Once again Ellie felt a wave of pure physical awareness in the closeness of his body to hers. His deep black hair was wind-swept and his eyes creased against the harsh glare of sun against ice. His dark skin seemed to merge into the ruggedness of this landscape, as if the land and this man were inextricably tied.

'You love it, don't you?' she prodded gently.

'Yes.' His tone was curt, as if admitting something that he didn't completely understand himself. He took a last long look around and started walking. Ellie followed.

'Why?' With a struggle she caught up to him and was trying to match his stride.

'It's hard to say.' He was talking to himself as much as to her. 'I was raised in Pittsburgh. My parents owned a farm in the south and we used to go there whenever we could. The contrast, the clean air, the lack of noise and the slowness of the pace, was unbelievable. And when I first read about the Antarctic I thought how much more so would be the contrast to an area where men had no place.'

'But men have a place here,' Ellie said softly. 'You're here.'

'I'm here because I have to be,' Leeton said abruptly. 'If the only people who show an interest in this place are those who want to develop it, then we'll lose it. The last true wilderness will be destroyed.'

Ellie shook her head. She was having trouble keeping up. 'This is crazy,' she said simply. 'I interviewed you in-depth two years ago and nothing of this came out.'

He raised his eyebrows. 'I didn't believe you were interested in anything more than my social life.'

She shrugged. She knew the readers of the *Daily* and she knew what they wanted.

'Why didn't you tell me about BIOMASS?' she demanded, still trying for the offensive.

'You didn't ask.'

Ellie took a deep breath. It was true. The first interview she'd had with Leeton—the one she had used to cover the social issues—she had carefully prepared for. The second—the one which took place the day after Sam's revelation—she had gone into unprepared and rigid with anger.

Sam's love of the high life—his betrayal of her so that he could move up the social ladder—had seemed in accord with Leeton Connor's lifestyle. Leeton's social set was what Sam aspired to join. It had seemed as if Ellie could no longer hurt Sam, but she had to strike out at someone. . .

The questions she had asked of Leeton's professional life had been shallow and ill-considered. As she'd asked them she had already formulated the article she wanted to write—an exposé of Connor's life of wealth and indolence.

'Not quite such a probing reporter as you thought, Dr Michaels?'

Ellie flushed. 'You don't feel totally committed to veterinary science,' she accused him. 'You can't main-

tain such a high profile and not enjoy it. Your cars. . .
your horses. . .'

'Is there anything wrong with my enjoying it?' Leeton
demanded. 'I believe I do. The only time I don't is
when Dr Ellie Coad puts her barbs into me in print.'

Ellie bit her lip and stared at the ice-flecked rocks.
What she had written was becoming more and more
indefensible. She stared down at her feet, concentrating
on keeping her footing on the treacherous surface. She
dared not raise her eyes to meet Leeton's.

'I would have said you were used to it,' she said
quietly. 'Heaven knows, you've been the subject of
media interest since you were born.'

'I should be,' he agreed pleasantly. 'It was inconsider-
ate of me to take offence, I'll grant you. You see, no
matter what else the media had printed about me, never
before had my personal integrity been slighted. And
your insults reflected on the work I was doing at the
time.'

'With BIOMASS?'

'Yes.'

'You could have told me you worked for them.'

'I intended to,' Leeton said bluntly. 'On the second
interview we'd arranged, you walked out after fifteen
minutes. As I recall, you pleaded illness. The sub-
sequent report on my professional life was a hotchpotch
of rumours and half-truths.'

Ellie bit her lip. 'I said I was sorry,' she whispered.

They had reached the edge of the ridge. Leeton
slowed to begin the rough climb down. Stepping on to
the first ledge, he held back his hand to steady Ellie.
She drew in her breath and withdrew her hand from his
proffered grasp. She had climbed up on her own; she
could descend on her own. This man's opinion of her
was making her feel about two feet tall.

He dropped his hand, raising his eyebrows sardoni-

cally. 'Have it as you like. As I said, it would give me
no great sorrow to see you break your neck.'

'You wouldn't get your precious publicity,' Ellie
snapped.

'There is that,' he agreed slowly. Then, as she
stumbled on the steep incline, he drew his brows
together. His hand came out and caught hers strongly
in his. As she pulled away his grip tightened.

'Submit, Dr Michaels,' he ordered. 'Or I'll carry
you,' he said grimly. 'And if you think I can't, I suggest
you keep refusing assistance and see what happens. If
you won't take care of your own neck, much as I dislike
the obligation, I'm compelled to do it for you.'

Ellie stared up at him. She gave her hand a half-
hearted wrench and Leeton's eyes lit with a gleam of
mocking laughter. He released her hand and pulled her
to him, ready to swing her up in his arms.

'N-no. . .' She wrenched back.

'Submit?'

'I submit. I submit. . .'

'Very wise.' He took her hand again.

Ellie stared down at the rocks. She couldn't see
Leeton's face, but she could hear the trace of laughter
in his voice. Her hand lay passive and supported within
his.

They walked on, moving swiftly from rock to rock. It
was easier moving with Leeton's support, Ellie conceded. The man had been walking over icy rocks for
twelve months and he moved with the agility of a
mountain goat. In comparison she was clumsy and
inept.

As they came around a curve close to the shoreline
Leeton came to a shudden halt. Taking advantage of his
momentary stillness, Ellie removed her hand. She
opened her mouth to comment — then saw why Leeton
had stopped.

Lying on a rock before them was a penguin chick, a

half-grown adelie. It was lying spread-eagled on the rock-face. Sensing their approach, it made a weak effort to move, then lay back exhausted.

Ellie made a tiny exclamation of dismay as Leeton bent over and lifted the little bird. His mouth was set into a grim line.

'What. . .what's wrong with it?' she asked.

'It's starving,' Leeton said. 'Something must have happened to its parents, or it's been separated from them somehow.' He felt the bird's slight frame then turned the little penguin over so that Ellie could see its eyes. 'The skuas don't waste much time,' he said softly.

'Oh, no.' Ellie's voice was a horrified whisper as she saw the damage the skuas had wreaked. She reached out and touched the soft chick down. 'Is. . .is there anything we can do?'

Leeton stared down at the bird and grimly shook his head. 'Nothing,' he said harshly.

'You can't. . .we can't just leave it here to die.' The memory of the men's attitude to the seal came flooding back.

'What are you suggesting?' Leeton demanded. 'That we take it back to camp and nurse it back to health? It's lost the sight of an eye. It's suffered massive weight loss. Only the fittest survive here, Ellie, and this bird will never be a hundred per cent fit.'

'It's not fatally hurt. You could save it. . .'

'Sure,' he agreed quietly. 'I have the vet skills to get it over shock, prevent infection and keep it alive. But in the wild, even if we did restore its health, it would never survive winter. And you don't turn birds which have been wild for thousands of generations into tame pets.'

'But we can't. . .'

Then Ellie's breath caught in her throat as she realised what Leeton was doing. His face was set and hard. He had made his decision and he was wasting no time. To wait was only prolonging the wounded bird's suffering. His fingers pressed hard down on the bird's throat, and his fingers were swift and sure. Seconds later he laid the lifeless body of the little bird back on to the rocks.

Ellie turned away. It seemed so unfair. . .

'The skuas can have him now,' Leeton said grimly. He looked over at Ellie and his mouth tightened. 'A hard lesson, Dr Michaels. This is a cruel continent. There's no room for weakness. The weak are doomed.'

'We could have. . .'

'Could have what?' Leeton said harshly. 'Could have nursed him back to health, and keep him as a pet for the rest of his life? What sort of fate is that? We're not here to interfere with the natural order of things, Ellie.'

'You interfered.'

'I know. I stitched the seal, but the seal was a healthy pup with a cut. Here I hurried nature along, and there are those who'd argue I shouldn't even have done that.'

Ellie fell silent. They walked on. 'I'm glad you did,' she said finally.

He grimaced. 'I couldn't do anything else,' he admitted. He smiled suddenly, his smile laced with pain, and Ellie knew for sure that the chick's death had upset him as much as it had her. 'My poodle streak,' he told her. 'And I'm really nice to old ladies.'

'I'll bet you are.' She tried to smile.

'Why did you work for the *Daily*?' Leeton asked suddenly.

'You've asked me that before.'

'And been told it's none of my business,' he agreed thoughtfully. 'You left there just after you wrote the article on me.'

'Before you had me sacked.'

'You over-estimate my influence.'

Ellie shrugged. Half of New York's media had Connor family backing. Even *Our Planet's Health* had Leeton Connor among its major shareholders.

'You didn't leave because of me, though, did you?' he continued, relentlessly pursuing his line of thought.

'No.'

He considered. 'Your husband left you and you wrote the article condemning me at the same time. Then you left the *Daily*. If the first two things are linked then the third has to be.'

'Whatever you say,' Ellie said uninterestedly.

'Will you marry again?' Again the question came from nowhere, catching her unawares. Before she had time to catch her thoughts, she had answered.

'No.'

'Why not?'

'Because I don't trust men,' she said harshly. Then, in counter-attack, she threw her own question. 'What about you, Dr Connor? When you get back from here, is one of those lovely ladies photographed so often on your arm going to make it as hostess of the Connor mansions for the next forty years?'

He raised his brows. 'I suppose so,' he said casually. 'If I can find one who meets requirements.'

Ellie laughed humourlessly. 'Poor girl.' She stumbled, and Leeton held out a hand. She backed off. 'No.'

He grasped her hand firmly in his. 'If you don't want to be carried, then learn to accept assistance with grace,' he ordered.

Her hand lay in his. Despite their thick gloves, warmth ran between them as a tangible link. Ellie felt her colour mounting. She looked up at Leeton. His cool grey eyes were watching her, appraising.

'Well, Dr Michaels, do I have a fight on my hands?'

She shook her head, not trusting herself to speak.

'A pity,' he mused. He tightened his grip and started to climb down.

No longer did Ellie have to depend on the soft rubber of her boots to grip the icy surface. At every step she was steadied, her safe path assured.

Her colour stayed high. The feel of his hand in hers was burning to her touch. Dear heaven, her treacherous mind thought, to be loved by such a man as this! To be cared for and cherished by Leeton Connor!

She gave a gasp as she realised where her thoughts were taking her, and Leeton looked back, his eyebrows raised in question.

'Is something wrong?'

'Nothing's wrong,' Ellie snapped. 'Let's go.'

He paused for a moment, looking down. The expression in his eyes was unreadable. It was almost as if he was seeing what was in her mind, Ellie thought bitterly. She gave her hand an angry tug, but his grip tightened. For a moment their gaze was locked together, angry brown eyes meeting calm grey ones.

'What's wrong, Dr Michaels? Don't you like being touched?'

'Not by you,' she said.

They were silent for the rest of the walk back. Ellie submitted to Leeton's assistance passively, with as much good grace as she could muster, and tried to block out the thought and feel of his hand touching hers.

Finally they rounded the last headland and the little camp came into view. Sven and Gordon were down at the shore with one of the inflatable boats ready to go.

'I thought you'd backed out of my algae-photographing expedition,' Gordon chided Ellie gently. His eyes fell and rested curiously on her and Leeton's linked hands. With Ellie's last angry tug Leeton finally relinquished his hold. 'Are you afraid?'

'Of course I'm not.'

'Maybe you should be.' Leeton was looking up at the sky and frowning. 'I don't like it,' he told Gordon. 'The weather's building up.'

'I know,' Gordon said. 'We may be in for a few rough days.' He looked across at Ellie. 'I think we should still go. It may be our last opportunity for a while.'

She nodded, biting her lip in exasperation at herself. No one was saying what was obvious. If she'd been back when she had promised the photography would have been done.

Leeton was shaking his head, his eyes on Gordon. 'I don't think you have time,' he said slowly. 'It's building fast. I'm sorry, Gordon, but it has to be cancelled for today.'

Gordon stared at him. 'But I need this photographed,' he said harshly.

'Then we wait for the storm to pass.' Leeton looked up again. 'Because we're sure as hell in for a storm.'

'He's right, Gordon.' Sven's soft, accented voice cut across the tension between the two men. 'You'd just get out and it would start to blow.' He turned to Leeton. 'I was trying to persuade him while you were away. He doesn't listen.'

'Because we're wasting time.' Gordon's voice was full of pent-up fury, far more than the occasion warranted. 'We're running out of time and I have so much to do. So much. . .'

'There's work to be done in the huts and you know it.' Leeton's voice was stern. 'You're not endangering your life and Dr Michaels' because you're in a hurry.'

'Are you pulling rank on me?'

'Yes, I am.'

The two men stared at each other. For one dreadful moment Ellie thought Gordon was going to strike out, and Sven made a movement to take his arm, but Leeton signalled him back.

'No, Sven. Gordon knows I'm right.'

Silence. Then Gordon swore and wheeled away. They stood and watched while he strode away over the rocks and behind the huts.

'Whew. . .!' Sven let out his breath in a long whistle. 'I thought he would do a murder.'

'He certainly wanted to.' Leeton was staring at

Gordon's retreating figure. 'What on earth is eating the man?'

Ellie stared down at her feet, saying nothing. Her heart was twisting inside for the angry man who had stormed away, and her guilt at depriving him of the morning in the boat was tearing her apart. Leeton looked down and caught her expression.

'You know something,' he said suddenly. 'Don't you?'

She shook her head. 'He hasn't told me anything,' she said. A tear came sliding down her cheek and she brushed it away angrily. 'But I should have been back. If you'll excuse me. . .' She followed Gordon up the slope until she reached her hut. Going inside, she closed the door carefully behind her, put hands to her face and wept.

'What the hell's going on?'

The threatening storm had broken with a vengeance. The men had spent an hour battening down the little camp, stringing the guide ropes between the huts and making sure all was secure. As the wind rose their work had become more difficult, and now there was nothing to do but to stay inside the beleaguered huts until the fury of the storm had worked itself out.

'What do you mean?'

'Why were you so upset?' Leeton was removing his snow-spattered outside gear and carefully shaking the snow on to a waterproof sheet. Ellie was seated on her bunk, her pen poised as it had been for the last hour. She had written exactly nothing.

'I should have been back,' she told him again. 'I destroyed Gordon's plans.'

'But there's time to spare for photographing algae,' Leeton said slowly.

'I know that. It's just that Gordon is under pressure and I didn't want to add to it.'

'Because he's depressed.'

'Mmm,' Ellie nodded non-committally.

Leeton stared at her. 'There's something you know that I don't,' he said finally.

She shook her head. 'Gordon has told me nothing,' she said quietly. 'I can make all the suppositions in the world at this stage, and that's all they are — suppositions. And talking about them is going to get us nowhere.'

Leeton continued looking down at her, baffled. Finally he shrugged. 'Well, I can hardly send him off to Kellent in this,' he said resignedly. Outside the wind was starting to scream and the hum of the steel cables made an eerie backdrop. 'And despite his anxiety to be out in the boat, we all have solid work to do inside, getting our results and samples in order for the trip home.'

Ellie nodded. She looked around at the mass of equipment stored in the hut. Trays of samples; jars of specimens and sheaf upon sheaf of roughly written notes. 'If they have as much as you they'll have their work cut out,' she agreed. She hesitated. The fact that Leeton's belongings had been piled up to make room for her bunk had not escaped her attention.

'I'm going to be in the way,' she said softly.

'Yes, Dr Michaels,' he agreed firmly. 'You are.'

They worked solidly through the day. Ellie stayed on her bunk, carefully out of the way of Leeton's methodical packing. The thought of Gordon in the next hut was very much with her, but she knew there was nothing she could do. He would let no one near.

Leeton had passed her a pile of research papers, and she waded through them carefully, trying to distract her mind with work.

The first articles she picked up were those he had done on the huskies, the dogs she had seen around Kellent. Ellie stared down at table after table of statistics — of results of blood tests and every other conceivable piece of information about the dogs.

'I don't understand what you're doing here,' she said softly as he looked up from the specimens he was sorting. 'Surely the dogs are the least important area of study for vets interested in Antarctic wildlife?'

Leeton shook his head. 'They're a real problem,' he said slowly. 'And one which will have to be resolved in the near future.'

'Why?'

'They're inbred,' he said briefly, 'to the point where genetic problems are starting to show. If you read the details you'll see what I mean. We're getting hip dysplasia and other disorders not seen in mainland huskies.'

'So increase the genetic pool,' Ellie said slowly.

Leeton shook his head. 'That's dangerous. It's bad enough having these dogs here because of the chances of cross-infection with the wildlife. There are all sorts of disorders that could cross over into the seal or even the bird populations. Every time we bring down another animal, the risk heightens. This place has been isolated for so many thousands of generations, there's been no natural immunity gained at all. Disease could decimate the entire continent.'

Ellie fell silent, going back to the sheafs of written research. The work Leeton had done on the genetic problems was now seen through new eyes.

'So what's the answer?' she said finally.

Leeton crossed to sit on the bunk next to her. He had folded his bunk to give him more room to work. 'I don't know,' he said heavily. 'Or perhaps I do know but I don't like it.'

Ellie nodded. 'No more dogs.'

'No more dogs,' he agreed. 'But it's hard. For men isolated here for months without family, dogs make the best therapy. For instance, what Gordon needs at the moment is a big hairy dog who'll sit and look at him with understanding eyes while he pours out his worries. I've watched the men during wintering over, and the dogs are a major source of comfort. With modern skidoos they're hardly needed for transport, but psychologically they're of major importance.'

'Man's needs or the needs of the Antarctic,' Ellie said slowly. 'Which is more important?'

Leeton shrugged. 'I'm not here to make that decision,' he said firmly. 'I'm here to find out the facts, and you're here to present them to as big a public as possible, so that everyone can have a part in decision-making and not just the people who stand to gain, like the oil companies and the tourist operators.'

'What would happen to the dogs if it's decided they can't stay?' Ellie asked quietly, knowing her readership and knowing that, however sensible the decision not to keep dogs, the emotive appeal of the dog's fate would be of paramount importance.

Leeton smiled. 'I'm way ahead of you,' he said. He pulled out another sheaf of paper. 'This details past dogs' acclimatisation to being taken away from here. It's a shock, but in fact most of the younger dogs can manage it. The older ones can't, and the plan at the moment is to let them live out their lives here, but do no more breeding. That's my recommendation. There are a couple of younger ones with major health problems — genetic disorders — and those will have to be put down within the next couple of years.' He shrugged. 'It's a matter of getting all bases to follow suit.'

'So no more Antarctic dogs. . .' Ellie thought back to the stories she had read of the dog sleds of the early explorers. 'It's the end of an era.'

'They haven't accepted my recommendations yet,' Leeton said drily.

Ellie read on, taking pages of notes as she did. As she worked she made a list of photographs she must take to accompany her stories. Before she left Kellent she must have film of the dogs, preferably a team working, she thought, as she stared down at the story she was creating.

'Does it worry you,' she asked Leeton curiously, 'that your research will have such a wide effect? Will it give you satisfaction to see the dogs removed?'

Leeton laughed without humour. 'You see me as a power broker, don't you, Dr Michaels?'

'Yes,' she said simply.

'Well, for your information, I don't like it,' he said harshly. 'I've watched the men with the dogs and I don't like what I'm having to recommend. But I have no other answer.'

Ellie bit her lip and bent again to her work.

The tension inside the little hut built up as the day progressed. Ellie found herself straining her ears, desperate to hear a drop in the level of the wind. If anything it was rising.

'I thought this was supposed to be summer,' she told Leeton after a compulsory trip to the 'bathroom'. She had been forced to make the trip holding the guide rope hand over hand. There was nothing outside but white, and if she turned in the wrong direction she could be lost four feet from the hut.

'We're getting to the end of the season,' Leeton told her. 'This is the Antarctic, after all. If the weather were dependable we'd be inundated with tourists.'

'Will it be clear by morning?'

He frowned over his work, clearly preoccupied. 'I shouldn't think so,' he said abstractedly. 'A storm of this magnitude will take a while to blow itself out.'

'Well, how long?' Ellie was staring at him.

'Two days, perhaps,' he said easily. 'Maybe three. It shouldn't be more. We've had storms blow for a fortnight, stop for a day and start up again. That's mid-winter, though.'

NO COST! NO OBLIGATION TO BUY!
NO PURCHASE NECESSARY!

PLAY "LUCKY 7"
AND GET AS MANY AS SIX FREE GIFTS...

HOW TO PLAY:

1 With a coin, carefully scratch off the silver box opposite. You will now be eligible to receive two or more FREE books, and possibly other gifts, depending on what is revealed beneath the scratch off area.

2 When you return this card, you'll receive specially selected Mills & Boon Romances. We'll send you the books and gifts you qualify for absolutely FREE, and at the same time we'll reserve you a subscription to our Reader Service.

3 If we don't hear from you within 10 days, we'll then send you four brand new Romances to read and enjoy every month for just £1.80 each, the same price as the books in the shops. There is no extra charge for postage and handling. There are no hidden extras.

4 When you join the Mills & Boon Reader Service, you'll also get our free monthly Newsletter, featuring author news, horoscopes, penfriends and competitions.

5 You are under no obligation, and may cancel or suspend your subscription at any time simply by writing to us.

You'll love your cuddly teddy. His brown eyes and cute face are sure to make you smile.

Play "Lucky 7"

Just scratch off the silver box with a coin.
Then check below to see which gifts you get.

YES! I have scratched off the silver box. Please send me all the gifts for which I qualify. I understand that I am under no obligation to purchase any books, as explained on the opposite page. I am over 18 years of age.

MS/MRS/MISS/MR _____ 6A3R

ADDRESS _____

_____

POSTCODE _____ SIGNATURE _____

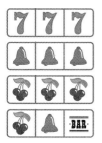

WORTH FOUR FREE BOOKS
FREE TEDDY BEAR AND MYSTERY GIFT

WORTH FOUR FREE BOOKS
AND MYSTERY GIFT

WORTH FOUR FREE BOOKS

WORTH TWO FREE BOOKS

MILLS & BOON "NO RISK" GUARANTEE

* You're not required to buy a single book!
* You must be completely satisfied or you may cancel at any time simply by writing to us. You will receive no more books; you'll have no further obligation.
* The free books and gifts you receive from this offer remain yours to keep no matter what you decide.

If offer details are missing, write to:
Mills & Boon Reader Service, P.O. Box 236, Croydon, Surrey CR9 9EL

Mills & Boon Reader Service
FREEPOST
P.O. Box 236
Croydon
Surrey
CR9 9EL

NO
STAMP
NEEDED

She closed her eyes, sighed and flopped back on to her bunk.

'What's the matter, Dr Michaels?' Leeton picked up another sheaf of paper and handed it to her. 'Haven't I given you enough work to do?'

Ellie glared at him and bent her head again to read.

Dinner that night was almost as tense as the first night. Leeton and Ellie fought their way through the wind to the other hut, having made a tactical decision not to eat in their own hut and intensify the intimacy. Sven greeted their decision with relief, and Ellie realised he was almost as tense as she.

Gordon said nothing during the meal, mechanically eating without enjoyment. His mood affected them all, and it was almost a relief to leave and return to their own hut. Once back, though, the tension between Ellie and Leeton continued to mount, and Ellie's concentration faded to almost nothing.

Finally she flung the paper she was working on aside. 'I've done enough,' she said decisively, glaring across at Leeton, who was still working.

'Can't take the pressure?' Leeton said drily, and she felt an almost overwhelming urge to throw something at him. He reached down and pulled out a box under the workbench. 'Have some light reading, then. It's mostly junk. Reading material gets scarce here, and people circulate whatever they've brought.'

Ellie swallowed her niggle of guilt and reached for the box. She was tired, but she wasn't going to sleep with Leeton still working. She might as well indulge. . .

She pulled the contents of the box on to her bunk and leafed through them uninterestedly. They were mostly motor magazines, science fiction or lurid Westerns — the sort of literature men used as bedtime reading after a day's hard physical work. Girlie magazines were conspicuously absent, and Ellie wondered if Leeton had removed them before her arrival. Probably not, she thought. It must have been Sven or Gordon. Leeton Connor was not going to worry about offending her sensibilities.

To her surprise there were a couple of women's magazines. An old issue of *High Life* topped the pile. Ellie looked at the cover. It was the issue immediately after Leeton had left to come down here. She flicked open the pages and Leeton Connor smiled out at her.

According to the paragraph beneath the photograph, he was at a farewell cocktail party. He was surrounded by a sea of expensively dressed, smiling people raising champagne glasses in his honour. At his side was a willowy blonde, exquisitely gowned and immaculately groomed. She was smiling possessively up at him and his arm was around her, holding her close.

For a long while Ellie sat and stared at the faces in the photograph. She knew these people. They were the people Sam had aspired to be associated with. These were the people she had rejected utterly when she had donned jeans and sought a job with *Our Planet's Health*. And Leeton Connor was one of them.

She threw the magazine back on to the pile, the old anger surging in her again. Looking up, she found Leeton's eyes resting on her face.

'What's wrong now?' she demanded. Reaching across, he picked up the magazine she had just discarded. He flicked it open, and saw immediately what she had seen.

'Why anger, Ellie?' His eyes were watchful, appraising. He held up the photograph she had seen. 'Why does this photo make you angry?'

'It doesn't.'

He raised his eyebrows in polite disbelief. 'You don't approve of the social set?'

'No,' she said stiffly. 'I don't.'

'Why not?'

She shrugged. 'My husband aspired to belong to your

crowd,' she said stiffly. 'He's still aspiring, as far as I know. Moving from woman to woman to achieve his ends. Like...'

'Like me,' Leeton said drily. His eyes were watchful. 'I see...'

'You don't see anything at all,' she snapped.

'Do you still love him, Ellie?'

She shook her head mutely and turned away. The hut was too small. She felt as if she was suffocating.

'I'm going to bed,' she said stiffly. 'You can stay up packing your nasty little specimens into jars. I'm tired.'

He said nothing, just stood, watching. Finally Ellie rose and made to brush past him.

'Where are you going?' he asked mildly.

'Where do you think I'm going?' she snapped. 'For a moonlight stroll? I'm going to the bathroom.'

'Not in a huff, you're not,' he told her firmly. She already had her hand on the door-handle. 'You'll take three extra minutes and rug up. This weather could kill you.'

By the time Ellie returned she had herself under control. Leeton was once again seated at the workbench, carefully sorting. Under his hands were his specimens of sea life, all carefully preserved. Ellie wrinkled her nose at the smell, and made straight for her bunk. She undressed with speed and slid under the covers, still recovering from the buffeting she had received on her small foray outside.

It was one thing going to bed — it was another entirely to go to sleep. She closed her eyes and resolutely counted sheep. She did her multiplication tables until nineteen times seventeen defeated her. She carefully blanked her mind until she felt fuzzy. Still sleep wouldn't come. Instead was a growing, aching awareness of the man at the bench.

Finally he too rose and made ready for bed. Sliding

down under the covers, he looked across at her tightly closed eyes and grinned.

'Having trouble, Ellie?'

'No.'

His grin deepened. 'Aren't you tired?'

'I'm very tired. I'm especially tired of talking.'

He nodded and twisted into a comfortable position. Ellie's bunk moved with his movement and she winced.

'What's happened since Sam, Ellie? Is there someone else on the scene back home?'

Ellie took a swift intake of breath. 'Mind your own business,' she muttered.

'You're always telling me that,' he complained. 'I spend my time answering your questions, and you won't answer mine.'

'You're not the least interested in me,' she snapped. 'You're only asking to taunt me.'

'Am I, then?' His tone was thoughtful. 'You know, I don't think that's right, Ellie Michaels.' He lifted a hand up and ran it lightly down the curve of her shoulder. 'On the contrary, you're beginning to interest me to an extraordinary degree.'

Ellie flinched away. 'Don't do that.'

'Why not?' The hand was still moving and she could feel the strength beneath the fingers. 'Have you sworn off men? Did Sam make you so bitter you're sworn to celibacy?'

'That's right.' She hunched her shoulder and turned into the pillow. 'Don't touch me.'

His hand fell still. The air between them was electric. 'Is that what you really want?' he said.

Silence.

'Go on, Ellie,' he said quietly. 'Tell me you really don't want me to touch you. Turn and look at me, and tell me that. Ellie?'

'I don't!' It was a muffled whisper.

'Turn and tell me,' he ordered. 'I need to see your face.'

Ellie didn't move. Then, before she knew what was happening, his hands were lifting her, bag and all, to lie facing him. With his hands still holding her, he met her look. His eyes were inches from hers. She could feel his warmth on her face.

She was like a rabbit caught in headlights that mesmerised. She made a futile effort to pull away, but it was only a token. Her eyes couldn't move.

'Tell me,' he said again.

She couldn't. It was as if she was drowning, sinking deeper and deeper into his calm grey eyes, coming closer and closer to this man, this. . .

She had drowned. His mouth was on hers and the world was lost. There was only Leeton.

The kiss lasted forever. His mouth covered hers, tasting the sweetness of her, exploring the softness of her lips. Her lips moved, wanting him, welcoming the strangeness of his tongue, tasting in return.

Her hands were imprisoned in her bag and she fought to free them, desperate to touch the strong contours of his face. Her body was screaming an urgent need — a need that had been building for two long years.

Oh, God, she wanted him! This was her place — her destiny. It was where it was right for her. Her mouth was his. Her body was his. If only he could take her. . .

What was she doing? A tiny grain of sense at the back of her head screamed out a warning. His hands were in her bra; his fingers caressing the satin-smooth skin of her breasts. Her nipples were taut, aching for his touch. And the tiny voice was growing.

You're one of many, it was saying. You may want him, but his desire is because you're the only woman in this place. The only woman. . .

In a minute, her body rejoined. I'll be sensible in a minute. She gave a soft moan and clung closer.

It was Leeton who broke. Out of the depths of their desire he found the strength to resist. One moment she was being kissed, being held and being loved. The next she lay back, dazed, not understanding what was happening. She stared up at him with pain-filled eyes and her stunned whisper was a plea.

'Leeton. . .'

He was staring down at her, and in the fading light his eyes reflected conflict, desire and disbelief.

'You want me. . .'

'I. . .'

She couldn't answer. The tiny voice at the back of her head built to a shout. She looked up at his face and saw his desire, and saw the disgust in himself at what he was doing. She gave a tiny gasp of dismay and shook her head.

'N. . .no.'

He stared at her as if he was seeing something he had never seen before. Any tenderness — any hint of warmth — was gone from his eyes.

'I thought not,' he said. He sat up and pulled his sweater over his head.

'What. . .what are you doing?'

'Leaving,' he said, and his voice was shaken. 'You're getting what you've wanted all along.'

'I don't understand.' Ellie's whispered words were hurt, bewildered, like a child whose security had suddenly been threatened. Her mind wouldn't work.

He was standing, pulling on trousers, boots, anorak. Then he was folding the bunk and stuffing the sleeping-bag into its holdall. Finally he turned back to her.

'Goodnight, Ellie.' He bent and kissed her, and this time his kiss was brutal, a harsh denial of the tenderness that had been between them moments earlier. 'I don't know what you want, or why you're doing this to me. And I don't know why the hell I can't look at you without wanting you. But you can play your games without me.'

And he was gone.

Ellie lay and stared into the half-light, her mind a whirl of searing emotion. What had happened to her? She put a finger up and traced where his lips had been.

She couldn't believe it. It was like a dream. He had wanted her, and she had accepted his need because it was the same as her own.

The same as her own? She shook her head into the dark, tears of reaction starting to slip down her cheeks. It wasn't the same as his at all, she told herself harshly. Leeton Connor had not been near a woman for twelve months and had turned to her as any man might in similar circumstances. And when she had responded with desire he had pulled back, as if stung.

And she? It was time she faced it, she thought bleakly. She was head over heels in love with Leeton Connor.

CHAPTER SEVEN

THE next two days were the most confused Ellie had ever spent. Confined to her steel apple while the Antarctic storm unleashed its fury on the outside world, she felt as if she was in some kind of time warp, isolated from the world completely.

What Gordon and Sven made of Leeton's midnight arrival to share their hut she didn't know. Neither of them commented, except for Sven's aside to Ellie while Gordon was momentarily out of earshot that it was a relief to have Lee to share the oppression of Gordon's black mood.

Ellie slept and breakfasted in her hut, but for other meals she made the difficult crossing to share her meal with the others. It was worth it. Left to herself she believed firmly that she would go mad.

Between her and Leeton there was icy courtesy. The blatant insults of her first arrival had ceased, but Leeton was clearly appalled at what had happened and was risking no recurrence. He came across to the hut after breakfast each morning and worked steadily, but their conversations were restricted to just that — work and icy civility.

Despite her emotional turmoil Ellie was getting some excellent work done. Walter had been right to send her down here. No interview held in pressured conditions back in New York could possibly achieve what she was learning from hours and hours spent confined in a ten-foot dome with Dr Connor. Her articles grew, were checked, verified, changed, discarded or accepted. Under her bunk lay a folder of finished work, which

Walter would kill for. It was good. It would be good for *Our Planet's Health* and for Dr Connor's cause.

'It's a pity this office doesn't run to a fax,' she said stiffly towards the end of the second day of confinement. 'Walter could use this stuff now. This month's issue will be pale in comparison to next month's.'

'You'll be back soon enough,' Leeton said grimly. 'Another week here and then a fortnight for the return journey.'

Ellie nodded, bent over her work and trying not to look up. 'I wouldn't want the magazine to wait any longer for these articles,' she said quietly.

Leeton picked up the papers she had just had him check and glanced through them once again. He nodded as if satisfied. 'Well, whatever else you are, you know your job,' he admitted.

'What do you mean?' she said softly.

He turned away. 'I think you know what I mean. It means that personally I don't trust you an inch. I'll be pleased to see the last of you, but at least I'll be satisfied that your work is good.'

She flushed and looked down. She was very close to tears. 'I don't understand.' It was a whisper.

He was staring at her bent head. Silence ran between them. Finally he sighed and put her article down.

'You revile me, you write an article that offends not only me but my friends and work colleagues, you lie to me and let me make love to you.' He shrugged. 'The moralist position? I hardly think so.'

'You think I'm out for what I can get?' The whisper was, if anything, softer.

'I don't know what to think.' Leeton ran his hand through his dark hair in an expression of weariness. 'But I'm starting to think I don't give a damn. I just want this over and you out of here. So let's get this work done.'

Ellie said nothing. She hunched over the photographs

she was sifting through and fought to hold back tears. There was nothing she could do to change this man's opinion of her. One day's uncontrollable anger two years ago had cost. . . Had cost her what?

Love? The word flew into her head and she let it drift. If she had not written the article, would Leeton Connor want her?

He would, she acknowledged. There was pure physical attraction running between them that even he could not ignore. But then Leeton Connor was attractive to many women, and Ellie was not his style. She thought back to the woman she had seen photographed with Leeton in *High Life*. That was the sort of woman Leeton Connor would marry. Not some environmentally conscious doctor who had no aspiration to be anything other than a social outcast. . .

She glanced at her watch and was relieved to see the time.

'I have to go,' she said stiffly. 'It's my turn to cook dinner tonight.'

'Don't let me stop you,' said Leeton.

Most of the cooking equipment and the large stove were in the other hut. Ellie approached the task with caution, investigating the ingredients to hand and hoping like crazy that there was something easy. Cooking wasn't one of her strong points. She had never found it satisfying to cook for one, and Sam had always preferred to eat out.

To her relief there was something that she was all too familiar with, and, to her embarrassment, Sven and Gordon were absurdly generous in their praise.

'You'd think I'd invented spaghetti and canned meat sauce!' Ellie protested.

Sven wiped the last morsel from his plate with the garlic bread that she had created from a frozen breadstick. 'It's almost as good as the cans my mother opened,' he declared.

'You don't have canned spaghetti in Sweden,' Ellie protested, and Sven grimaced.

'Don't you believe it,' he said darkly. 'If it's easy then my mother has found it. If it's as convenient as spaghetti and meat sauce she will take a trip to Italy to buy it. In one-ton lots,' he grinned.

'It's not bad.' The comment came from Gordon. To Ellie's delight Gordon had actually eaten most of his meal. The storm was showing signs of abating and his mood of black depression was lifting. He cast a wicked look at Leeton. 'If I were you I'd marry the girl,' he declared. 'With skills like this a man couldn't go wrong.'

'Marry her yourself,' Leeton said shortly, and Ellie flushed.

She excused herself as soon as she reasonably could. Her little hut was lonely, but it was better than being near Leeton. And if she couldn't find sleep at least she could let her aching head lie on the pillow and dream of what might have been if she hadn't written that accursed article.

She slept at last, and woke to silence. The wind had disappeared. For the first time since Ellie's arrival, even the cables anchoring the hut to the ground had ceased to hum.

Outside, the world was white and still. Ellie opened the door slowly to avoid snow falling inwards and looked out to sunlight. It was so bright after the dullness of the past two days that it physically hurt. The silence was so absolute that it was almost eerie. The grey of the rocks had temporarily disappeared.

'You'll see the rocks again by nightfall.' Leeton appeared from behind the hut and his words in the silence made her start. 'At this time of the year the snow at the shoreline disappears fast.'

Ellie nodded, her mind only half on what he was saying. The enforced confinement in the hut had enabled her to cover nearly all her written work. Now she was aching to get back to her photography.

'Thank you for the information,' she said politely, and turned away.

He watched her curiously. 'Not in a seductive mood this morning, Dr Michaels?'

Ellie gasped. Her eyes flashed up to meet his, and anger met anger. How dared he. . .?

Without thinking she bent and seized as much snow as her hands could hold and hurled it with all her might at the man before her. The soft, dry snow sprayed out over him, covering him with white.

'Well, well.' The words were almost of satisfaction. 'Is this the temper I know so well?'

Ellie threw another handful. Her rage was almost choking her. Then as the snow hit him full in the face he decided to retaliate. The world was lost in a hail of white. Her efforts to spray Leeton were lost as his spray of snow engulfed her.

He was coming towards her, and there was nothing she could do about it. The dark shape grew closer, the snow pelting in a thickening torrent. Finally he reached her and her hands were stilled by his grasp.

'Enough,' he ordered. 'Surrender.'

Ellie struggled uselessly against his iron clasp. 'Let me alone,' she choked. 'You. . .you. . .'

He looked down at the snow-covered girl he was holding and his mouth twisted. 'Don't you know what I am either, Ellie?' he asked grimly. Then he smiled, and his smile was dangerous. 'But at least you have to accept your place. There's only one answer to insubordination in this camp,' he told her severely. He loosened his grip on her hands, but before she could escape he had reached around and swung her up into his arms.

'You need some cooling off,' he told her.

'Put me down.'

'I intend to,' he told her firmly. He was looking

methodically around the camp. 'It's just a matter of finding somewhere suitable.' His gaze fell on the side of one of the huts, where the soft snow had mounded in a vast pile. 'I think I may have found just the spot.'

'Leeton Connor. . .' Ellie's voice was a squeak. 'You wouldn't. . .'

He shook his head sadly. 'Dr Michaels, your trust in human nature does you credit, but I'm afraid it's sadly misplaced. This is Dr Leeton Connor you're talking to, remember. And surely you have no illusions as to what *he* is capable of.'

While he was talking he had taken the few short steps to the mound. Ellie was lifted high in his arms and then dropped firmly to disappear in a sea of white. She emerged, spluttering and fighting, to find she had an audience. Not only Leeton but Sven and Gordon were standing watching the emergence of the white-frosted girl from her burial mound.

'You'd think a qualified doctor would have more dignity,' Leeton said mournfully. 'No wonder you wouldn't let her look at your hand, Gordon. She looks about ten.'

'You have a blob of snow on your nose, Dr Michaels,' Gordon told her. 'And a larger one on your head, and a couple in each ear. . .'

'Thank you.' Ellie glared at them all. 'I hope you have to sleep with your rotten fish specimens under your bunks all the way back to Tasmania!'

With the good weather the mood of oppression lifted from the camp. There was work to be done, and apart from meals and sleeping the huts were never used. Gordon's depression lifted and even Leeton and Ellie were able to be civil to each other. The sleeping arrangements didn't revert to Leeton and Ellie sharing a hut. By mutual consent the topic of doing so was not even raised.

Still the icy formality was retained, and Ellie was starting to believe it would stay like that until the end. She watched the easy camaraderie Leeton had with Gordon and Sven, and her heart twisted in jealousy. These men are his friends, she thought. Why can't I be?

You don't want to be a friend to Leeton Connor, her evil voice told her. You want to be much, much more. And you're pipe-dreaming like a silly teenager with a crush. . .

The sea had been stirred up by the storm, so it was not until four days afterwards that the little boat was finally launched on to the cove. Even then Leeton was not completely happy.

'Gordon, there's a real rip running towards the left of the cove,' he said. He had stood watching the water for half an hour before Sven and Gordon had brought the inflatable dinghy down to the shoreline. 'And the wind's rising. Why not wait until tomorrow?'

'I've run out of tomorrows,' Gordon said harshly. 'Tomorrow we have to start breaking camp and you know it, Lee. Besides, it may well be no better.' He stood and stared at the water. 'It's fine. You worry too much.'

Leeton frowned. 'Why don't you content yourself with the sheet ice being washed against the rocks?'

'The thin ice that I want breaks up as it hits the thicker ice at the edge of the cove,' Gordon said patiently. 'I want Ellie to photograph large sections, with the light coming through the thin ice. For heaven's sake, Lee, don't interfere this time. I'll keep the boat running towards the right,' he added.

'Maybe.' Leeton's frown remained unchanged. He looked across to Ellie. 'You don't have to go unless you want to.'

'I know that,' Ellie said quietly. It wasn't true,

though. She wasn't going to hinder Gordon's plans a second time.

Leeton's expression was of someone allowing something to happen against his will. Clearly, though, he too didn't want to interfere with Gordon again.

'You'll both wear immersion suits,' he said harshly.

'They hamper movement,' Gordon protested.

Leeton shook his head. 'Immersion suits or the whole thing's off. And for God's sake, Gordon, be careful.'

Gordon laughed, able to smile now he knew Leeton was not going to prevent the trip. 'Do you think I'd sink us?' he demanded. 'I'd get my photographs wet!'

Ellie joined in the laughter, but at the expression on Leeton's face a niggle of doubt grew in her mind. She slipped on her immersion suit and felt comforted rather than impeded by its sheer bulk.

Sven and Gordon helped push the inflatable out into the water. They stood on the shore, watching for a few moments. As Ellie looked back over the water they finally left the occupants of the boat to their own devices and returned to camp.

Soon the little grey boat was out in the middle of the cove. Around the boat was clear water, with the occasional sheet of thin ice floating past.

'I need to collect some samples from the bottom of the cove first,' Gordon said. He produced a mechanical grab which he organised over the side.

Ellie was free to sit and take in the scenery. She needed to do so. Leeton's reservations had communicated themselves to her and she was having trouble coping with her nerves. Still, it seemed as if Gordon had been right. There was no danger. . .

The weak sun shone on her face. The wind was cold, but in her bulky immersion suit she was comfortable. The motor putted quietly behind them, keeping the little boat away from the shore with its jagged ice. While Gordon worked, Ellie held the nose of the boat into the wind, a simple task which exactly suited her state of mind.

Finally Gordon had the samples he wanted.

'OK,' he said briefly. 'Now let's find some algae.'

It was harder than he expected. The wind was rising, driving the loose sheets of ice against the rocky sides of the cove. Here there was danger to the little boat. A jagged piece of loose ice in the open sea would brush against the thick rubber and cause no harm. When the ice was against the rocks, however, or packed against more ice, the boat could be holed as the ice was driven into its side.

They negotiated as close as they dared, and Gordon reached over to haul in a sheet of the thin ice. He turned it over, exposing a murky film of algae for Ellie to photograph. She took several shots from different angles before she was satisfied, finding, as Leeton had told her, that it was a far different experience from photographing microscopic subjects in the comfort of indoors. Then, as Gordon turned to search for more ice, the motor on their tiny rubber craft spluttered and died.

For a moment they sat looking at each other. Then Gordon swore heavily and reached for the starter button. Nothing.

Ellie pushed the jagged piece of ice she had been photographing back into the water and reached for the oars. Three more attempts on the starter button and Gordon abandoned the motor. He grabbed the oars from Ellie's inexpert grasp and started to row.

The slurry of ice around the boat and the force of the wind prevented them from making any headway at all.

Ellie glanced desperately towards the shore from where they had been launched. High on the hill above the camp was a tiny figure. Leeton? Or Sven? It shouldn't matter. One of them would be watching. Suddenly, though, it seemed absurdly important that the watching figure be Leeton.

'The boat's going to be holed,' Gordon said desperately. 'With our weight in it and the wind driving it against the ice it doesn't stand a chance. We're going to have to get out.'

'Get out?' Ellie's composure had disintegrated. She was unashamedly terrified.

Gordon motioned to the larger ice-floes between them and the rocky sides of the inlet. 'They should hold our weight.'

'You have to be kidding!'

Gordon shook his head. 'I wish I was,' he said, grimly. 'OK, Ellie, me first.'

Ellie watched in horror as he swung himself over the side of the boat, on to the ice-floe that the boat was wedged against. The floe sank a couple of inches but remained stable. Gordon reached back in and seized a rope tied to the front of the boat.

'Now you,' he said urgently. 'You get out and we tow the boat back.'

He moved carefully on to the next floe, leaving the original ice for Ellie to climb on to.

For a moment she sat numb. What Gordon was proposing seemed crazy. Then she looked down at the jagged edges of the ice pressing into the rubber sides of the boat. Any minute now one of those edges would pierce the rubber and she would have no choice. On top of that they would have lost the boat. She shoved her camera quickly into its waterproof covering, slung it around her neck and followed Gordon.

The floes were slippery and awash from the waves, sinking as they stepped on to each and tilting as they manoeuvred their bodies from one side to another. Manoeuvred was the right word, Ellie thought grimly. She didn't make any attempt to walk; her motion resembled something between a crawl and a slither. Crossing from one floe to the other seemed impossibly difficult. Behind them came the boat, bumping along

the floes behind them, no longer in danger with its
weight removed and dragged along by the rope around
Gordon's wrist.

Ellie found she was shaking. Her teeth were chattering uncontrollably. Although she was cold it was fear
that was making her body react. The rubber immersion
suit was still keeping her dry.

She didn't see Gordon fall. One moment he was on
the floe in front of her, standing to assess the stability of
the next floe; the next he had simply disappeared from
view. Ellie looked up from the ice where she had been
concentrating on finding a hand-hold and realised that
he was no longer there.

The floe in front of her was large and humped. It took
her only seconds to realise that Gordon must have
slipped into the water on the other side of the mounded
ice. Abandoning her fear in the face of her terror for
Gordon, Ellie shoved herself hard on to the humped
floe. Gordon was in the water, his immersion suit
holding him buoyant.

He was trying frantically to gain a hand-hold on the
slippery floe, his face contorted with fear. For a
moment — a fraction of a second — Ellie didn't understand, then as she saw what Gordon had seen her body
froze in horror. On the rocks above the cove was the
huge bull leopard seal. Its channel to the open sea was
the water where Gordon was floundering, and it had
clearly decided the only course of action was to attack
this strange creature invading its territory.

Surely it wouldn't attack? Please, God. . . Ellie
stretched out full length on the ice-floe, took Gordon's
hand in hers and pulled.

He couldn't get enough grip to slide on to the ice. As
she moved to get a better grip herself the seal slid into
the water, under a floe, and came straight for him.

Gordon screamed. His face contorted with agony.
Letting go his grip on Ellie's hand, he swung his bulky

body round to try to drive off the thing that was gripping his rubber-clad suit.

Ellie was kneeling up, sobbing with fear and in-decision. Then, as Gordon swung around in the water, thrashing wildly, she saw the seal exposed above the surface. Almost instinctively she hauled the heavy camera from around her neck, whirled it high on its strap and crashed it down on the seal's head. The camera and skull met with a sickening thud. As they did, Ellie overbalanced on the precarious ice and slid slowly into the water.

Whatever she had done to the seal, at least it was no longer threatening. She and Gordon were alone in the water.

Gordon's face was grey with shock and pain. Ellie reached forward to support him.

'Gordon!' Her voice was harsh as she tried desper-ately to reach into his consciousness. 'Gordon, it's all right. It's gone—the seal's gone.'

Her words registered. He looked at her dully. Already his body was less buoyant. The seal had punctured his suit and the freezing water would be oozing in. He floated passively while Ellie twisted him around, linking her hands under his arms and across his chest. She looked frantically around. How was she going to get him out of the water?

She was no longer on her own. On the shore near the huts two figures were desperately working to inflate a second boat. As she watched, the boat was shoved into the water, heading towards her and Gordon at full power.

Leeton was alone in the boat. For a moment Ellie wondered why Sven hadn't come too, but then realised that the little boat couldn't hold four. In her arms Gordon was growing heavier and she felt her own suit being dragged down with his weight.

'Let me go.' Gordon's voice was slurred and indistinct. 'I'll pull you down.'

'Shut up,' Ellie said fiercely in what she hoped was her best bedside manner. Then, 'Gordon? Do you still have the rope?'

On the other side of the ice-floe Leeton had reached the side of their dinghy. If Gordon still had the rope. . .

He had. He had wound it around his wrist while he negotiated the floes. It was still there. Ellie reached forward and looped it around her own wrist, then held it up for Leeton to see.

He got her message at once. 'Hold on,' he called, and his voice was cracked with anxiety. Ellie closed her eyes as the strain of doing just that took its toll. She had no intention of doing anything else.

The next few moments were a blur. Somehow Leeton attached his boat to the incapacitated dinghy and manoeuvred it slowly, cautiously, out into the open water. Behind it came the rope, with Ellie and Gordon still attached.

Somehow they got past the jagged ice. Ellie had no free hand to fend off the sharp edges. Once a piece ripped into her shoulder, and she felt a sharp pain, then a rush of cold. She pushed her body sideways so that the tear was out of the water, and went back to grimly hanging on.

Finally they were clear. With his motor still running, Leeton turned the disabled boat until he could grip the rope. From there it was only seconds until they had Gordon's inert body in the boat. Then Leeton's strong hands reached down and lifted Ellie under the arms, up and in. The motor was gunned into gear, and the little boat turned and headed fast back to shore.

Ellie did not relax. The most important thing was to get Gordon back where he could be warmed, but meanwhile the blood loss had to be checked. Beneath the ripped rubber of Gordon's suit his leg was a gory mess.

She needed a pad. She looked around the boat, searching, her mind turning over possibilities. Then she pulled back her immersion suit, hauled off her already wet sweater and worked it into a pad. Leeton made a motion of protest, but the sweater was off before he realised what she was doing. Ellie shoved her arms back into her suit while she worked. The wind was cruel.

By the time the boat beached, she had a pad hard around Sven's leg, with some of the rope from the bottom of the boat tying it tightly into place. Blood was already seeping through.

Sven was waiting for them, striding into the water to pull the boat out. His normally ruddy face was white with shock and concern.

'I've radioed Kellent,' he said briefly. 'The LARC is on its way.' He looked briefly down at Gordon. 'I thought it best to mobilise them and call it off if we didn't need them. . .' His face tightened and he stooped to help lift his friend. It was obvious to all of them that help was very much needed. Between them, Leeton and Sven lifted Gordon from the boat and carried him up the beach to the first hut. Ellie was left to follow.

By the time she had rid herself of her immersion suit and followed them into the hut, the men were ridding Gordon of his sodden clothing and were rubbing him mercilessly. The water had been freezing. The sub-zero temperature was enough to kill him, let alone the shock of blood loss.

'Don't touch his leg,' Ellie said urgently. Her rough binding was still intact. 'Leave it for me. . .' Her voice shook and faltered and she stopped.

First things first. Leaving Gordon to the men for a moment, Ellie stripped off her wet undershirt and hauled on another sweater. Her arm was bleeding sluggishly, but she ignored it. Her teeth were chattering uncontrollably as well, and if she didn't attend to herself she knew she stood a strong chance of going into shock. Then she turned to Gordon's ashen form.

In the corner of the hut was her medical bag. Leeton was foraging through the top layer and held up an ampoule of morphine. Ellie nodded, and Leeton moved to administer it.

'Hot-water bottles?' she demanded. 'Do we have such things?'

'Yes. The water's heating in the other hut,' Sven told her.

'Go and fill them,' Ellie ordered. 'Even if the water's only lukewarm it's better than nothing.' She looked down at Gordon in indecision. He was close to unconsciousness. 'Let's rug him up,' she told Leeton.

Gordon was lying on top of Leeton's sleeping-bag. It was open, so it was a matter of pulling it around him and zipping it closed. As Sven returned with water bottles Ellie slid two down against his sides. Then, with Leeton's help, she sliced the base of the bag, allowing her access to strap a wad of dry padding to the injured leg. A couple more bottles were placed inside against his feet and the slit in the bag pulled together.

'Do you have saline in your bag?' Leeton's voice was clipped and businesslike and his fingers were on Gordon's pulse. 'His blood-pressure. . .' With relief Ellie realised that she wasn't a doctor alone in a crisis. She had a colleague.

'Yes.' She had already stooped to her capacious medical bag. 'Stephen Ryde thought it was foolish to have me here unprepared.' She gave a rueful grimace. 'I thought he was being over-zealous. I owe him an apology.'

Leeton nodded, his hands already lifting the saline bag from Ellie's grasp and placing it on a shelf above Gordon. Ellie turned with the syringe, searching for a vein, but to her dismay her hands wouldn't stay steady.

She placed the needle near Gordon's skin and then drew back.

'I. . . I can't,' she said. 'My hands won't work.'

Leeton gave her a brief, hard glance and took the needle from her grasp. 'I can do this on a budgerigar,' he said firmly. 'Gordon should be a pushover.'

'If I moult I'll sue.' Gordon's voice was a thread of a whisper, but it made them all smile. The needle slid home with ease and the drip was set.

'Gordon, you have a huge gash on your leg that needs stitching, and you're suffering from hypothermia,' Ellie told him, trying to keep the tremor from her voice. 'We can't take care of you here. The LARC's coming over from the mainland to pick you up. Dr Ryde and I will take care of you once you're at the base.'

'As long as it's not the budgie doctor.' Gordon's voice was fading to nothing, and Ellie's eyes creased in concern.

The door of the hut opened and Sven appeared. 'The LARC's at the entrance to the cove,' he told them. He stared down at Gordon. 'He is going to be all right, isn't he?' he demanded from Ellie, and she took a deep breath before answering.

'Of course,' she said, and her words were meant to reassure Gordon as well as Sven. 'We'll get him warm and stitched and he'll boast of his heroic fight with a leopard seal for the rest of his days.'

'There's blood on your sweater.'

Leeton swivelled at Sven's words. The fresh sweater Ellie had pushed on was stained with her blood.

'I assumed it was Gordon's,' Leeton said angrily. 'Why didn't you tell us?'

She made a gesture of impatience. 'It's nothing,' she said swiftly. 'I'll have Stephen look at it back at Kellent.'

Leeton moved to lift her sweater, but Ellie backed off. 'I'm fine, Dr Connor,' she snapped. 'We don't have time for fussing. The LARC's waiting and I want Gordon down there. Now.'

They glared at each other for a fraction of a second, but Ellie was right and Leeton knew it. The patient in danger was Gordon.

Ten minutes later they were down at the cove again. There was an inflatable dinghy on the shore, bigger than those Ellie had seen previously. A burly bearded man was waiting on the shoreline as they carried Gordon down, and at the entrance of the cove a LARC was standing just offshore.

They had not moved Gordon. Ellie had repacked the sodden pad around his leg, wincing as she realised the extent of the damage, then placed more bedding around him. With him cocooned in his sleeping-bag, with water bottles intact, they had simply carried the bunk in its entirety down to the cove. It made an excellent stretcher. To her relief Ellie saw that it would fit into the dinghy and Gordon wouldn't have to be further disturbed.

'Doc Ryde's in the LARC,' the bearded man told them.

'I'll have to go too,' Ellie said briefly. Gordon's leg was a mess and Stephen Ryde was going to need more than his plumber-anaesthetist to assist him.

Leeton nodded. 'Sven and I will pack up and come over tomorrow,' he said briefly. 'We're as near finished that it'll make no difference.'

'We haven't photographed the skuas.' Gordon's eyes were open. The morphine was taking effect and his voice was blurred with the drug.

'I'll personally photograph your beloved skuas,' Leeton promised.

'You!' Gordon's weak voice was scornful. 'You couldn't photograph kittens.'

Leeton grinned and bent to lift the stretcher into the little boat. Before she knew it, Ellie was out on the cove again. Once again Leeton and Sven stood on the shore watching them go.

Her time at Morrag was over. Ellie shook her head in disbelief. She looked back at the two diminishing figures on the shoreline. Her time with Leeton Connor was over.

There was no time for reflection. For the time being, her time as a journalist was over as well. For now her other self was required. Taking a deep breath, Dr Ellie Michaels turned to tend to her patient.

CHAPTER EIGHT

ELLIE woke to warmth. She lay for a moment, savouring the luxury, then slowly opened her eyes. She was in a strange bunk in unfamiliar surroundings. The events of the past few hours came flooding back to her, and she closed her eyes again.

To her annoyance, Stephen Ryde had taken one look at her and treated her as a patient.

'I'm going to need you, Dr Michaels, and you're no use to me if you're dead of shock yourself. You're nigh on freezing, and that arm needs stitching.'

Ellie had protested fiercely, anxious that Gordon get Stephen's full attention, but the older doctor had insisted.

'There's not a lot I can do for that leg until he's warm and out of shock,' he confessed. 'I might as well concentrate on getting you into a fit condition to help me.'

So Ellie's arm was attended to and she was bundled into bed with a pain-killer for her arm, a sedative and as many hot-water bottles as could be wedged around her slight form. She had fallen asleep protesting.

Her eyes opened again and she pulled her wrist from the covers. Her small waterproof watch was still going, and she resolved to send a letter of gratitude to the manufacturers as soon as she returned to New York. Some claims really were true.

She had slept for four hours. It was late afternoon. She stirred languorously under the covers, soaking in the delicious warmth. As she did, the door opened and Stephen came in. His face cleared when he saw she was awake.

'Feeling better?'

'A thousand per cent,' she smiled. 'Thank you.'

He waved an airy hand. 'Don't mention it — all part of the service. Besides, your fee will be settled by hard labour. We have a tricky piece of surgery on our hands.'

Ellie nodded. 'I didn't see much,' she admitted. 'But what I did see I didn't like.'

'There's deep tissue and muscular damage,' Stephen said briefly. 'Associated nerve damage, I'd guess. And it's not going to wait until we can evacuate him out of here.' He looked down at Ellie. 'It's us or nothing, I'm afraid, my dear.'

'I thought you'd say that,' Ellie smiled. 'I guess this means I have to get up.'

'If you're up to it,' he said. He hesitated. 'Ellie, there's something else.'

'Oh?' Her eyes were watchful.

'I've just done a full check. Gordon has a classic crop of Kaposi's sarcoma.'

Ellie was silent. Seated on the bunk beside her, Stephen Ryde watched her face. 'You don't seem surprised,' he said quietly.

She shook her head. 'I guessed AIDS was a possibility a few days ago.'

Stephen nodded. 'When I saw the sarcoma I pulled out Gordon's history. He was involved in a car accident five years ago. Major trauma — he would have received massive blood transfusions.' The big doctor grimaced. 'He must have been given infected blood. Nothing else fits. We do a thorough screening before anyone's allowed down here, pulling out any risk factors, but I guess no one thought of this one. Maybe we should have, but we don't test for HIV.'

Ellie bit her lip. 'Some people are born unlucky,' she said, almost under her breath. She found a tear was sliding down her cheek, but she didn't check it. It seemed so damned unfair.

'Will this affect how we treat him?' she asked quietly.

Dr Ryde shook his head. 'Of course not,' he said definitely. 'With luck he'll respond to AZT once he gets home and will have a few more years of active life. We fix this leg. It means we have to double-glove and take a bit more care during surgery, though.'

Ellie nodded. 'He doesn't want it known,' she said quietly.

'I can understand that,' said Stephen, nodding. 'Some people are almost unbelievable in their paranoia of the disease, and it's impossible to guess where the paranoia will crop up. We don't need to tell anyone. If just you and I operate. . .' He fell silent.

Ellie stared at him. 'There's something else?' she asked quietly, watching his face.

'Mmm.'

Silence. It was as if he didn't want to go on. Finally he seemed to come to some decision. He looked down at the slight girl huddled in her cocoon of warmth and wished he was anywhere but here. Still, what had to be said needed to be said now. It couldn't be put off.

'Ellie, that slash on your arm—can you be sure it wasn't touched by any of Gordon's blood?'

Ellie met his look. She thought back to her blood-stained hands pulling off her sweater. 'No,' she said.

'You've thought of it?'

She nodded slowly. 'If you mean did I know the risks when I was trying to stop him bleeding, I guess I did. There certainly wasn't time to go and don double gloves and protective clothing, though. And the risk is minimal.'

'It's still there. . .'

'If I treat a patient with meningitis there's a tiny risk that I'll catch meningitis,' she said harshly. 'It doesn't mean I don't treat that patient.'

Stephen nodded as though she had given the answer he wanted to hear. 'And Leeton and Sven?'

'I was the only one who touched his leg. Leeton may have in the boat, but he was wearing gloves.'

Stephen sighed and stood up. 'So it's only you who has to worry.' He shrugged. 'A minor worry, I concede, but still it's a worry you could do without. You now have a window period of six weeks before you can be checked. It means that, apart from Gordon, you're not going to be able to practise as a doctor.'

'I'm a journalist anyway,' Ellie smiled. 'Remember?'

Stephen smiled, but the worry was still behind his eyes. 'You're a doctor,' he said quietly. 'Whatever your reasons for playing at being something else, Dr Michaels, the woman I'm looking at is still a doctor at heart. And a damned good one. . .'

He hesitated. 'At least you have a nice quiet sea voyage before you,' he continued softly. 'And I'm afraid if you have a boyfriend waiting in New York you're going to have to greet him very chastely until the window period is up.'

Ellie stared at him, then grimaced. 'You needn't worry, Dr Ryde,' she assured him. 'My love life is the least of my problems.'

The surgery on Gordon's leg was performed late that evening. Ellie was impressed with the efficiency of the tiny theatre. Because of the size restrictions of the room, they worked without help. The same surgery back in New York would be done with the back-up of a full nursing team, but Ellie and Stephen coped alone.

'And it prevents complications,' Stephen said wryly. 'If Gordon wants his secret kept I'm darned if I can think of a reason to tell an assistant why we have to be so damned careful with the swabs.'

It was a couple of years since Ellie had given an anaesthetic, and she was grateful for Stephen's barked instructions. The man was skilled and efficient, and she watched with admiration while the leg was meticulously repaired.

'He'll have a rip-snorter of a scar,' Stephen told her as they washed afterwards. 'I'm no plastic surgeon.'

'You're some surgeon, though,' Ellie said in admiration. 'Gordon's been lucky.'

'Hah!' said Stephen.

Afterwards, Ellie sat with Gordon until he woke. It was late; most of the camp had gone to bed. Gordon had the sick-bay to himself, a tiny room with two bunks lying feet apart. Ellie sat on the other bunk, leafing through magazines, her mind on a thousand things beside the glossy articles she was staring at. Finally Gordon opened his eyes.

'Hi,' Ellie said softly, smiling down at him. 'Welcome back.'

He grimaced, moved slightly and winced. 'Where the hell am I?'

'We're at Kellent.' She smiled. 'Still in the Antarctic, I'm afraid. If I had a magic wand I'd spirit us out of here, but we're stuck.'

He was silent, and Ellie let him be. She picked up her magazine again, to take the pressure to talk away from him.

'It feels as if I still have a leg down there.' His tone was cautious.

'A leg with a magnificent scar, but a leg for all that,' she agreed. 'Dr Ryde's done a great job. You should have no problems.'

Silence. Finally Ellie put down her magazine. 'Would you like me to fetch you a drink?' she said quietly.

'No.' He stared at her. 'Ellie. . . Dr Michaels. . .'

'Ellie,' she said firmly.

He closed his eyes. 'I should have told you,' he said harshly. 'Before you operated, I mean. I. . . It was all those damned drugs. I was half asleep from the time I got the first shot. . .'

'It doesn't matter.'

He winced. 'Ellie, I have AIDS.'

'I know,' she said gently.

'But you operated. . .'

'And Dr Ryde and I took full precautions,' she reassured him.

His brow cleared. 'I thought. . . I hoped you knew,' he said. 'And Dr Ryde. . . Did you tell him?'

'You have Kaposi's sarcoma,' Ellie told him. 'Stephen guessed all by himself.'

'Oh, God.' He fell silent. Finally he stirred again.

'I wouldn't have come if I thought I'd really get full-blown AIDS,' he said tiredly. 'I knew I was HIV-positive, but I treated it as a future worry. In ten years it might worry me. Not now.'

'I can understand that.'

'Can you?' He looked up at her and what he saw seemed to reassure him. 'You're not frightened of treating me?'

Ellie shook her head definitely. 'Of course I'm not.' She grinned. 'I'd be a lot more frightened if I were treating you for chickenpox, and I've even treated that in my day. Despite the fact that I'm a sitting duck for chickenpox.'

He gave a rueful smile. 'And you didn't tell anyone else?'

'I didn't. And neither did Stephen.'

He sighed and stirred restlessly. Ellie picked up a syringe and filled it with morphine. 'Dope time,' she said firmly.

'I suppose you think I'm stupid for not telling anyone,' he said fretfully. 'Especially now that I have definite signs. Like the sarcoma.' He sighed. 'I. . . I just want to go home and have everyone pleased to see me. I don't want people treating me like a tragedy before I am one.'

'I can understand that as well.' Ellie pulled back his

covers, swabbed his arm and found the vein. She injected the needle with care.

He took her hand. 'You won't tell. . .you don't have to tell Lee,' he asked, his voice shaking. 'Or Sven. . .'

Ellie shook her head. 'Dr Ryde knows and I know — that's it. I think you're underestimating Lee and Sven, but I promise no one will hear from us.'

He fell back on to the pillows. 'Thank you,' he said simply. 'And I'm sorry. I would have told you if I could. I wouldn't have willingly put you at risk. . .' He grimaced. 'If you double-gloved you should be OK. It's only if there's blood transfer. . .an open cut. . .' His voice slurred to silence and his eyes closed. He was asleep.

'I don't want him told about my arm.' Ellie was bidding goodnight to Dr Ryde. 'He has enough to worry about without having me on his conscience. He doesn't have to know that I even scratched myself. You're the only one who knows it was deep. Everyone else can think it was just a scratch, and Gordon doesn't need to hear about it at all.'

'I don't like deception,' Stephen said slowly. 'But I think you're right. . .'

Leeton and Sven arrived the next day. The LARC brought them over towards nightfall, having made two previous trips to dismantle the camp and bring it back to base. As the LARC approached base for the last time Ellie was standing on the shore to greet them.

Sven was first off the LARC. He jumped from the bow on to the rocky shore and seized Ellie's hands between his. Then he let them go, spread his arms and enveloped her in a bear-hug.

'You are OK? They tell me you are OK. It is true? And Gordon?'

'I'm really OK,' Ellie smiled. She was warmed by the exuberance of his greeting. 'And Gordon's fine too. Not quite up to standing on the beach to greet you but anxious to see you for all that. He's in sick-bay waiting.'

Sven didn't need telling twice. With a happy grin he sallied forth, and Ellie looked affectionately after him. Sven was on his way home to his beloved wife and two little girls. His research was done. His friends were fine and he was happy. She turned back to find that Leeton also had swung himself out of the boat.

'So, Dr Michaels.' His tone was wary.

'Dr Connor.' The words were absurdly formal.

All she wanted to do was to fling herself on his chest and weep. And he stood there, surrounded by the bustle of unloading, by men hauling the last traces of the Morrag camp from the LARC, and made no move to even smile. Ellie felt chilled to the bone.

'Your arm?'

'A scratch,' she lied. 'Stephen saw to it.' She was feeling an almost overwhelming compulsion to share the shadow hanging over her with this man, but his coldness checked her. Besides, AIDS was Gordon's nightmare. It was not hers, please God. And she had promised Gordon her silence. She gave an involuntary shiver and turned away.

'Ellie.'

She stopped but did not turn back.

'You saved Gordon's life,' he said formally. 'I should thank you.'

'There's no need to thank me,' she said savagely. 'I would have done the same for anyone.' She took a deep breath. 'Even for you, Dr Connor.'

She walked back into the buildings, leaving him staring after her.

There were three days left to them at Kellent, before they were to board the *Ice Maiden* for the journey north and home. The packing up at Morrag had only been brought forward two days, so little had been left undone there.

To her delight, when the last unloading from Morrag was done and Ellie's belongings restored to her, a battered camera was included. She picked it up and examined it cautiously. The casing was smashed but the waterproof cover seemed intact. Holding her breath, she locked herself into the tiny cupboard which the base personnel used as a darkroom. The film was undamaged.

'Where on earth was it?' She went to find Sven, her hands full of perfect algae photographs. If anything could cheer Gordon, these would.

'I'm not responsible,' Sven told her. He grinned. 'It was lying on an ice-floe — near where your friend the leopard seal introduced himself. We saw it through the binoculars and Lee said he would try to get it.'

'Lee. . .'

'Crazy, huh?' Sven demanded. 'He went alone because it breaks every rule in the book to have both in the one boat and no one on shore.' He hesitated. 'It breaks every rule in the book to be in the boat when there are just two at the camp. But he tried.' He grinned. 'I'm glad the photographs worked,' he told her. 'I hope they were worth the risk.'

'He did that. . .'

'And you know the weird thing?' Sven said. 'The thing that makes me say to Lee he is crazy. Your friend the seal is back in his position, exactly the same, watching, watching. Only this time he must have a very sore head. I tell Lee it is like the crocodile in *Peter Pan* — he tastes human and he wants more.' Sven shrugged. 'The man is crazy, as I tell you.' Sven was watching Ellie as he talked, his kindly eyes seeing more than she would wish. 'Or a little bit in love, I think.'

She flinched. 'That's nonsense,' she said. She stared

down at the photographs. 'Gordon must see these,' she said stiffly. 'It'll almost make his sore leg worthwhile.'

Gordon was sitting up in bed when she entered the sick-bay. Beside him, with sheafs of written notes in his hands, was Leeton.

'I'm sorry,' Ellie said awkwardly as she realised Gordon was not alone. 'I'll come back later.'

Leeton has already stood. 'No,' he said, still formally. 'I was just going.'

Ellie nodded and stood back to let him pass. He gathered papers from the bed and turned. Then he glanced down at the photographs she was carrying.

'Anything of interest?' he enquired mildly.

She hesitated, then nodded again. Leeton had gone to considerable trouble to fetch her camera. It was petty of her to deprive him of seeing the results.

'The algae,' she said softly. She came forward and spread the shots over Gordon's counterpane.

They were wonderful, the blue-green algae as a soft film over the wafer-thin ice. Ellie had taken them with the sea as a background. The sunlight glinted through the ice and bounced back from the rippling salt water. If anything could make the algae look beautiful it was these photographs.

Gordon passed from photograph to photograph, his eyes lighting and the deep mantle of depression lifting as they watched. His fingers shook as they lifted each shot. Finally he looked up at Ellie. 'They're bloody magnificent,' he whispered. 'They'll get me what I want.'

Ellie smiled. 'Which is what?' she said. But Gordon was bent again over the photographs and was in a world of his own. It was left to Leeton to answer.

'Apart from Gordon's weird obsession with the skuas——' this brought a swift, wry grin from the man in the bed '——he's been working almost exclusively with algae. It's damned important. The algae bloom occurring during ice melt means food for the krill. The krill, in turn, are the major food of five species of whale, three of seal, twenty of fish and many of birds — including penguins. The huge swarms of krill allow even the whales to feed efficiently, but if anything interferes with the algae, and thus the krill, all of those species face extinction.'

Ellie nodded. She picked up the photographs. 'Thank you for rescuing my camera, then,' she said stiffly. 'It seems it was worthwhile.'

'I believe I did it for Gordon,' said Leeton, just as formally. 'And for our research.'

'Of course.'

They stayed glaring at each other, and Gordon laughed. His laugh was the most carefree Ellie had heard from him.

'They're fantastic, Ellie,' he told her. He turned to Leeton. 'And did you photograph my skuas?'

'I did.' Leeton sighed and dug his hands into his trouser pockets. 'Probably not as effectively as our Dr Michaels would have, though.'

'Well, there are some here,' Gordon said. 'Ellie, will you take some photographs out at the dump? We have to show the bad as well as the good.'

Ellie nodded. 'I can do that.'

'Show her the effects of the rubbish on the birds,' Gordon told Leeton.

Leeton's eyes were still. OK,' he said, without expression.

'Well, go on.' Gordon waved an airy hand. 'I'd come myself, but my domineering doctor won't let me get out of bed.'

Ellie grinned at him, delighted in the change the photographs had wrought. 'Yes, sir,' she said.

Leeton and Ellie donned coats and walked together out to where the rubbish was mounded in a great heap behind the camp. Ellie's nose wrinkled in distaste. This was the ugly side of this magic place.

Here the skuas foraged methodically through the garbage. Discarded machine parts and other trash was piled high, creating not only an eyesore but a hazard to the wildlife. Ellie raised her camera and took photographs while Leeton foraged among the garbage. Finally he lifted a gloved hand, bearing aloft a dead skua. He laid it on a piece of rock and waited while Ellie crossed to see.

The bird had choked on a piece of plastic. A sliver of plastic still hung from its beak. Leeton stared away into the distance, while Ellie raised her camera.

'Photograph it well,' he said harshly.

She cast a quick, nervous glance at him and went back to her camera. This man was an enigma to her. In his voice was anger, more anger than at anything she had ever done to him. It was anger at the futile death of an ugly bird.

Finally she finished. Lowering the camera, she looked nervously up at him.

'I need to photograph the dogs,' she said quietly.

He nodded, already starting to walk away. 'They're chained on the other side of the base,' he told her.

There were eight dogs, and they greeted Leeton with a volley of frantic barking. He moved down the line of the long-haired huskies, greeting every dog by name. They wriggled ecstatically under his hand, then barked urgently as he moved away. Ellie put her hands to her ears at the din.

'They're bored,' Leeton told her. 'They're working dogs. Unfortunately there's no work for them to do, and we can't leave them unchained because of their risk to the penguins.'

Ellie nodded, her camera already working.

'I'll have the men harness a sled this afternoon,' he told her. 'You can see what they can do then.'

He had reached the end of the line. A young dog was under his hand, squirming with delight. Ellie watched as Leeton unclipped the dog's chain and let it free.

'Have you seen a glacier?' he demanded suddenly.

'I. . . No.' Ellie's voice was uncertain.

Leeton looked down at the dog. 'This is Marbuck,' he told her. 'The Curtin Glacier is only half an hour's trek from here, and Marbuck would love a run.' He ran a hand over the dog's smooth coat. 'Wouldn't you, boy?'

The dog responded with frantic affection. Behind them, the other dogs barked in jealousy.

'They're all exercised,' Leeton told Ellie, following her eyes. 'Every time they can, the men take one out. But no more than one, because we can't keep a check on them. I'm not going to be responsible for their wanton killing of the penguins.' He rose from his stooped position. 'Get anything you need,' he said firmly. 'We start in five minutes.'

'I don't. . .'

'I know,' he said grimly. 'You don't want to spend any more time with me. Well, the feeling's mutual. But I want publicity for this place, Dr Michaels, and I'm prepared to put aside personal wishes to obtain that. So get moving.'

CHAPTER NINE

THEIR journey around the coastline to the glacier was done mainly in silence. They followed a worn route — obvious the glacier was a major attraction for those with time on their hands during the summer months — but today they had the track to themselves. Most of the occupants of Kellent were making last-minute preparations for the ship's departure the next day. Even those staying for the winter were getting their last mail ready for posting.

Around their feet, Marbuck raced and barked and raced again, streaming ahead of them until he was a speck in the middle distance, checking to a halt and then tearing back to them as if his life depended on it. Ellie found herself bubbling with laughter at the antics of the pup.

'What will happen to him?' she asked.

Leeton smiled, the first genuine smile she had seen for the time they had been walking. He clicked his fingers and the dog came to heel.

'Guess?' he said.

Ellie stared across at him. Her jaw dropped and she started laughing. 'I don't believe it,' she said. 'There must be easier ways of getting yourself a dog. First, go to the Antarctic, second, persuade everyone there that the dogs are no longer to be kept, thirdly, arrange quarantine or immigration or whatever and finally teach your dog to live in New York.' She grinned again and raised her camera. 'Our readers will love it. Leeton Connor as a soft touch — they won't believe it!'

He smiled again, but the smile was a trifle rueful. 'It's

research,' he said firmly. 'How a dog born in these environs adapts to a much different climate.'

Ellie nodded. 'And totally necessary,' she agreed gravely, trying to keep the laughter from her voice. 'Your notes tell of the offers you've had from zoos and research establishments. All the dogs have offers of placement.'

'Well, they can't go to ordinary homes. They need to be carefully monitored while they adapt.'

She smiled again. 'I see.' She was unable to resist teasing. 'So you're only offering to care for Marbuck for science.' She stooped down and gave the bouncing Marbuck a quick hug. 'Marbuck,' she told him gravely, 'I'm sorry to have to tell you this, but your new master is a complete fraud.'

She glanced across at Leeton, bit her lip then gazed again at the track in front. She hadn't even drawn a smile. The man was unapproachable.

They followed the deep tracks of a bulldozer in the mushy, melting ice. The tracks were partly obscured by the snow which had fallen in the storm a week earlier.

'The weather's turning,' Leeton commented. Ellie's teasing was ignored. 'This snow would have melted a fortnight ago.'

Ellie didn't answer. Her cheeky riposte had left her breathless and slightly humiliated. Why couldn't she make him laugh? He walked and talked as if they were strangers, and communication could never build.

The sadness inside her was building, like a leaden weight. Beside her, Leeton's pace was brisk and businesslike. This journey seemed something he wanted to get over fast. Ellie was having trouble keeping up with both him and his dog.

Sensing her difficulty, Leeton looked over and slowed his pace slightly. 'It might have helped if you'd been fitter before coming down here,' he said curtly.

It was as if he was deliberately continuing to try and

hurt her. She glared at him, her anger coming to her aid. 'It might have helped if I'd grown another head higher,' she snapped. 'Your stride equals my trot.'

As they neared the glacier they struck inland. They climbed a barren, rocky ridge, and, before them, lay the Curtin Glacier.

All other thoughts were swept aside. The sight before them made Ellie catch her breath in wonder. The massive river of ice swept to the horizon, miles and miles of unbroken grandeur, inching its way to the sea. The glacier where they stood was over a mile wide.

Ellie couldn't drag her eyes from the sight. She had heard this landscape described as 'appalling', and now she knew how the person speaking had felt. Its vastness, its bleakness. . .

She shook her head. It was as if she had gone to sleep and awoken on another planet, a planet as inhospitable and barren as anything she had ever envisaged. Its very bleakness was beauty.

She raised her camera to her eyes and lowered it again. She had no idea how to photograph such a sight as this.

Leeton was watching her, his eyes hooded and assessing. 'Well, Dr Michaels? How are you going to capture this?'

'I can't,' Ellie said frankly. 'I don't think anyone ever could.' She shook her head. 'It would be crazy to try.'

'So the world doesn't get to see a glacier?'

She closed her eyes, trying to understand what she was feeling.

'I can't put this in people's living-rooms,' she said quietly. 'Not as I'm seeing it. In fact, I'm starting to wonder whether I even have the right to stand here and look.' She took a deep breath, feeling the bitter cold in her lungs. 'Nature's gone to such an amazing amount of trouble to keep people away. Should we even be here?'

Leeton laughed without humour. 'Try telling that to

the governments who think there's oil here,' he said harshly. 'Or the tour operators who want to develop it.'

They were silent again.

Ellie looked down. She knew that somehow she should try to take pictures. She would probably never be given another chance.

'Can we go on to the ice?'

Leeton nodded, then unslung a rope from his shoulder. He clipped one end on to her and the other to him in harness fashion.

'What's this for?' Ellie asked dubiously. The feel of him touching her was unnerving.

He was adjusting the rope to his satisfaction. 'Rules,' he said shortly. 'The glaciers have cracks in them. The cracks are what's generally known as crevasses, and some of them are thousands of feet deep.'

'But we'd see them.' Ellie looked nervously at the surface of the glacier.

He nodded. 'We should. In full sun, like today, they're relatively easy to see.' He frowned. 'All the same, there's still a lot of loose snow. Soft snow often banks and forms a roof or snow bridge over a crevasse,' he explained.

'I'll be careful,' she promised. With the rope now attaching them loosely together they moved apart and made their way to where the rocks dropped to ice. Marbuck was already careering crazily across the ice.

'Shouldn't we rope him too?' Ellie asked.

'The dogs seem to have a sixth sense as far as glaciers go,' Leeton told her. 'And they're lighter.'

The surface of the glacier was smooth and fairly snow-free. They walked for a few hundred yards out on to the ice before Ellie paused, looking back. Behind her Leeton stopped as well, waiting.

Ellie's breathlessness had only increased. Her whole body was caught in a limbo of unreality. This couldn't be her, Ellie Michaels, standing in this place with this man.

She looked back at Leeton. His face was creased against the biting wind. He was looking 'upriver' as if he too was trying to come to terms with the awesomeness of the place.

Dear God, she loved him. This man, this place. . . The two were intertwined in her mind. Leeton Connor, solitary and unreachable. How could she touch his heart?

She couldn't, she reminded herself savagely. She was as alone as he was.

The camera untouched, she turned to go back. There was no use standing here, waiting to find a way to photograph this place, to come to terms with it. She shook her head savagely, trying to understand. The Antarctic. . . Leeton Connor. . . There was no way she could capture either, in film or in any other form. Leeton's face was as bleak and as uncompromising as the landscape.

Suddenly the soundlessness of the place was shattered. As Ellie turned, the total silence was smashed into a crashing explosion. Noise smashed around them in waves, surging in massive echoes. Ellie stared in horror. Thunderous noise enveloped them from everywhere. It was impossible to define its source.

'What. . .what. . .?' Her terrified whisper was drowned by the sounds around them. The whole place was alive with echoes of the massive boom.

Leeton stood still, listening, as the wave of sound slowly receded. Finally the last echoes of the boom faded gradually away.

'I think an iceberg's just been born,' he said slowly.

'An iceberg. . .'

'Part of the glacier's just crashed into the sea,' he said. 'It's like a river. When it reaches the sea it falls away.'

Then, beneath their feet, the ice trembled.

'Let's get out of here,' Leeton said abruptly. 'Fast!' He gave a swift whistle. From hundreds of yards away over the ice, Marbuck looked across. Even from this distance Ellie could sense the dog's confusion and disorientation. Leeton whistled again and the dog took its first tentative steps forward. As he did the ice trembled again.

'Move!' Leeton's voice rang out harshly over the ice.

'Wh—why?' Even as she asked Ellie was already running over the slippery ice towards the bank.

'We're too close to the sea.' Leeton was exerting pressure on her end of the rope, hauling her ruthlessly along. 'The iceberg breaking away will result in pressure changes in this ice.'

The ice moved again as they hit the bank. Leeton sprang on to rocks and turned to haul Ellie the last few feet as a crack of shattering ice broke the silence and the ice split.

It seemed to happen in slow motion. Ellie had time to gain a foothold on a rock and turn, before the smooth white surface of the ice cracked neatly in two. It was as if a knife had sliced cleanly through the white frosting. One minute the ice was smooth and unbroken, the next a jagged fissure had sliced cleanly through, leaving a chasm that went down forever.

Ellie stared in stunned amazement, then in horror as she saw what was happening. Marbuck was trying to reach them. As the ice cracked he stopped dead. There was a high-pitched, terrified yelp and the ice under Marbuck's paws split in two. The dog disappeared downward.

Ellie took an involuntary step forward, but Leeton's grip held her like iron. 'No,' he said harshly. 'Wait.'

The river of ice was still moving, creaking and shifting like a living thing. They stood helpless, waiting for it to settle.

Finally it was still. Silence returned. There was nothing again but a river of ice, inching its way to the sea.

Leeton grimaced. 'It could be years before that happens again,' he said, almost under his breath.

'Marbuck. . .'

He glanced down at her, then across the ice. His harsh, hooded expression betrayed no emotion.

'Gone,' he said softly. And Ellie, staring up at him, knew that he was as distressed as she was.

'Could we see?' She stared across at the newly opened crevasse.

'It'll drop hundreds of feet,' Leeton said. 'A chasm as wide as that. . .' And then he stopped as if struck. From below the level of the ice came a high-pitched whine.

Ellie started forward and Leeton's hand came out to grip her. 'No.'

'We can't. . .' Ellie looked wildly out to the ice. 'We can't just leave him there.'

'No,' Leeton said again. He was swiftly unwinding the length of rope from over his shoulder. Some of it had been taken up between his and Ellie's harness. The rest was looped in large coils. He untwisted it and looked around until he saw what he was looking for — a large, jagged boulder at the edge of the glacier, with a relatively narrow base. Swiftly he looped the rope around the base and knotted it. Then he checked his harness and started walking backwards out on to the snow.

Ellie watched with horror. Leeton was walking slowly, feeling his way as he went. In his hand he carried his ice-pick. Before each foot went down, the surface of the ice was tested.

Finally he reached the edge of the gaping chasm. Here he dropped to lie full-length in the snow, inching his way forward until he was looking over the edge of the drop.

He stayed in that position for so long that Ellie was

close to weeping in frustration. Later she discovered that her nails had drawn blood by digging into her palms inside her mittens. She was desperate to call out, but equally afraid to shatter Leeton's concentration.

Finally he drew away from the edge. Drawing his rope in as he came, he returned slowly to where she stood.

'Well?'

He shook his head. His face was pale and defeated. 'It's no good,' he said.

'But I can hear him.' The dog's soft whining was all around them in the absolute stillness.

'Not for long.' Leeton sank down on a rock and stared out over the ice. 'He's caught on a ledge fifteen feet down.'

'Then we can get him. We can go back to base and get help. . .'

He shook his head. 'The ledge he's on is thin and fragile — I'm amazed it's held till now. The dog's injured and lying still, but the heat of his body is going to melt that ledge long before we can get back to base and return with the proper equipment to pull him out.'

Ellie was staring at him wildly. 'But we can't just leave him there.'

'We have no choice,' Leeton said coldly. He closed his eyes. 'It'll be fast, at any rate. Once that ledge goes. . .'

Ellie flinched, then she took a deep breath. 'Put the harness back on me,' she said, more firmly than she felt. 'I'll go down and pull him out.'

Leeton was staring at her as if she had taken leave of her senses. 'Don't be stupid,' he said. 'You'd never get up again.'

'You can pull me,' she said desperately. 'Don't you see? I'm light and the dog's only a pup. If you anchored the rope and then pulled you could do it.'

'And if I couldn't?'

'You can,' she said savagely. 'You can at least try. And you can at least pull me. If we're too heavy then I drop Marbuck and you just pull me up, but at least this way we've given it our best shot.'

'Our best shot. . .' He was staring at her as if he had never seen her before. 'And what happens if the ice closes?' His face was expressionless.

'Then I get squashed,' Ellie said frankly. 'I'm not like Sven, Dr Connor. I haven't a family depending on me. My life is my own and no one gives a damn about me anyway. No one's going to be all that heartbroken if I do get squashed. But I'm not going to leave here without having a go. Now will you help or won't you?'

His eyes didn't leave her face, and a twisted smile played on his mouth. 'The heroic Dr Michaels. . .'

'Just shut up,' she said desperately. Now she had made the decision to go down, the thought of the ledge melting and breaking away while they argued was more than she could bear.

'Yes, ma'am,' he said.

It was all very well talking big, Ellie thought, as she reached the edge of the crevasse. The difference between talking and doing was immense.

She was full-length on the ice, looking down. She could make out the pup, sprawled on his precarious ledge just beneath her. Beneath the pup was nothing — just endless black.

If she kept thinking she couldn't do it. The rope holding her was taut. Leeton had twisted it around the rock, letting out one loop at a time. She could feel his strength holding her and wondered fleetingly if she could attempt what she was doing with some other man at the end of the rope.

Absolute trust, she thought bitterly. That was what she had learned she could place in this man. And he had none in her. With one stupid article, she had destroyed any measure of trust he could ever have. . .

She was delaying the moment. She took a deep breath, turned and slid back over the edge of the chasm. The rope swung. She hadn't counted on the rope swinging. It destroyed her orientation. The blue-white ice was flashing back and forth across her eyes. She gave a sob of terror, closed her eyes and concentrated on keeping absolutely still until the swaying stopped.

Finally it did. As Leeton felt it settle he let out a fraction more rope and she started the downward journey. The dog didn't move. The whole world, it seemed, was holding its breath, waiting. . .

Waiting for what? Catastrophe? Ellie felt her mind fill with panic and had to close her eyes again for a moment as she fought for reason. There was one man and one rope between her and eternity. The thought was enough to make her hysterical.

Only there wasn't time for hysterics. An inch down, and then another. Ellie felt the ledge with her foot and pushed out past it, suppressing the urge to gain a foothold. With her weight the ledge would crumble. She let her hand hang down, inching nearer and nearer to the waiting pup.

Marbuck raised his head to greet her. He must have been winded in the fall. As Ellie's fingers searched to grasp his collar he struggled and tried to rise, and as he did the ledge crumbled and fell away. Ellie's fingers hooked into the collar and jerked the dog into her body, gripping fiercely with both hands.

The swaying went on forever. How Leeton held on she would never know. The sudden movement and the extra weight must have torn him in two. There was nothing she could do now. She closed her eyes again, willing herself to be still, and willing strength into the man above. He would know by the extra weight that she had the dog. Now it was up to him.

Slowly they inched upwards. Ellie couldn't look. She kept her eyes tight closed, fear turning her to stone. For an awful moment she had a vision of the rope fraying against the chasm's edge. Her eyes tightened further and she uttered a tiny whimper of pure terror. In her arms the dog lay completely passive, as if he too sensed that stillness was their only hope.

How was Leeton doing it? Any minute Ellie expected the rope to cease rising; for the order to release the dog from her arms. It didn't come. Slowly, slowly she was rising. Then the rope jerked and was still.

Ellie raised her eyes and opened them a fraction — just a fraction. Three feet above her head was the edge of the crevasse. So close. . .

She was praying silently under her breath, clinging desperately to the limp form of the dog. 'Please don't make me drop him,' she was pleading. 'Please don't. . .'

'Ellie, I've anchored you for a moment.' Leeton's voice was hoarse and tight with strain. 'Just hold on.'

Thirty seconds — a minute. Then the rope moved slightly and the upward motion started again.

Then she felt the edge. Her head was up, almost clear. Holding the dog with one hand, she reached up to find purchase. Her fingers slipped and the dog moved involuntarily. Ellie grasped Marbuck again with both hands and held on. Leeton was going to have to do it all on his own.

An inch. Another. Then her shoulders were up and over and her hands could somehow lift the dead weight of the dog up and out of the gaping chasm. She pushed him back away from the edge.

With the dog's weight gone, the rope holding her harness gained a new life. With a surge of strength, Leeton hauled her the last couple of feet, over the edge and out of the abyss.

The flat surface of the ice was heaven. Ellie lay full-length, her face against the snow and warm tears running down her cheeks. Beside her lay Marbuck, whimpering and crawling in to gain comfort from her body warmth.

'Ellie!' It was a rasping order. 'It's not finished yet. Pick up the dog and get off the ice.'

Ellie looked up wonderingly. On the bank of the glacier stood Leeton, the rope still stretched taut in his hands. 'Move,' he told her. 'Now!'

She nodded, numb with reaction. She knelt, cradled the pup in her arms and stumbled the last few feet over the ice, then the rocks were under her feet and Leeton had her in his arms.

Between them was the pup, but it was as if he were part of them. The three of them were locked together, and a song of joy was echoing around all three. Ellie was crying openly, the tears unchecked. She didn't care. She was alive and Marbuck was safe and Leeton had her in his arms, and heaven was here, now. She didn't move — none of them did. It was enough that they were safe and they were together.

Marbuck was the first to recover. He stirred in Ellie's arms, then raised his face to lick the nose she had pressed against Leeton's chest. Leeton felt the movement and pulled back to see.

'Well, well.' His tone was full of tenderness and wonder. He put a hand on the dog's shaggy head, but his eyes were still on Ellie.

'I think. . . I think he's hurt,' she whispered, her whole being alight to his look.

'Let's see.' He took the dog from her and laid him down on the snow. The dog looked adoringly up at him, his expression one of absolute trust. It was as if he knew what Leeton had done, Ellie thought wonderingly. Absolute devotion. Me and Marbuck both. . .

She caught at herself, her mind still dizzy with reaction, and sat down suddenly on the snow.

'Are you all right?' Leeton cast a quick searching

glance up at her while his fingers expertly ran over the dog.

'Nothing a good fit of hysterics wouldn't cure,' Ellie smiled. 'I've never been so terrified in my whole life.'

His eyes held her. 'Nor I,' he said slowly. He put a hand up and cupped it gently under her chin. His touch was a caress. 'Nor I.'

Ellie stared, her colour mounting. The touch of his fingers was sending shards of love through and through her. On the snow the dog stirred and whimpered, as if it knew their attention was gone. Leeton smiled and looked down. His hands kept on with their examination.

The dog's rear leg caught his attention. As Leeton touched it the dog whimpered again, and Leeton's fingers became gentler. He ran them down along the curve of the leg and nodded as though verifying something he suspected.

'He's fractured the lower leg,' Leeton said quietly, patting the dog softly on the head. 'And he's split his pad.'

'He won't. . .he won't have to be put down?'

He grinned. 'I wouldn't dream of doing such a thing,' he told her. 'If this dog's worth a life. . .'

Ellie flushed. 'It wasn't a risk,' she said slowly. 'I trusted you.'

Silence. The silence stretched out forever. Then Leeton's hands came up to take her face between them.

'Ellie. . .'

'Ellie! Leeton!'

It was a shout from the track behind them. Leeton let go of Ellie's face, but pulled her in beside him. His arm held her protectively as Sven and a party of others came running over the rocks towards them. Below the ridge, one of Kellent's sturdy four-wheel-drive vehicles was parked, and the men were moving towards them with haste.

Sven reached them first. By the time he arrived they

were standing waiting for him. As Ellie stood, her legs sagged beneath her. Reaction was settling in fast. She would have fallen, but Leeton's arm held her steady against him. He smiled down her, and his smile was full of warmth and reassurance.

'Our taxi,' he said softly. 'And it's just what the doctor ordered, I think. Or the vet. I wasn't relishing carrying both you and Marbuck home.'

'I can walk.' Ellie attempted dignity, but Leeton just grinned and held her closer. 'I'm sure you can, jelly-legs,' he teased. Then he turned to greet Sven.

Sven's white face told them of his concern even before he opened his mouth. In line with the rules of the base, Leeton had recorded the planned route and estimated time of their trek. The roar of the iceberg breaking away, combined with their now late return, would have led those at Kellent to fear the worst.

A few swift words and Leeton explained what had happened. Sven listened, open-mouthed with amazement. His eyes went from Ellie to the dog, to Leeton and back to Ellie. He made to say something, then thought better of it. Reaching across, he removed Ellie from Leeton's clasp and hugged her hard.

'Assuredly you should have been a vet,' he told her. 'You are quite mad. To do what you did for an animal. . .' He shook his head in wonder and grinned up at Leeton. 'She is as mad as you,' he told him.

The other men followed Sven. They had come prepared for a tragedy, and their faces exuded relief. Despite Sven's comments Ellie was not considered crazy. To her amazement her behaviour seemed entirely logical, and she knew that if each of them had been small enough to be capable of doing what she had done they wouldn't have hesitated.

For the first time she realised how cohesive the isolation of this place made the men and women here.

The dogs were part of their team, and thus part of them. And Ellie's action had also made her part of that team.

She stood silent, as questions and exclamations bombarded them. Too much had happened too quickly for her to be able to absorb it. The trauma with Gordon, and now this. . . Her arm still ached from the jagged cut it had received three days ago, and the pull of the harness had made it throb.

She leaned heavily on Leeton, his arm back supporting her, as voices rose and fell without meaning. She was where she wanted to be. Nothing else mattered. Finally Leeton signalled that it was time to stop.

'We need to get Ellie home,' he said gently, looking down at her white face. 'I think she's had enough.'

Ellie had indeed had enough. Reaction was making her whole body tremble. The rope had cut in under her arms and around her chest, and her body was starting to ache.

Sven moved to swing her up into his arms for the brief trip down to the truck, but Leeton stopped him.

'You take Marbuck,' he said, quietly but firmly. 'Dr Michaels is mine.'

CHAPTER TEN

THEY left Kellent the next day.

The base was a hive of activity. Ellie had hardly seen Leeton since their arrival back at the base. She had been taken in charge by Dr Ryde, and when Leeton had uttered a protest at having Ellie removed from his care he had been firmly put in his place.

'We have a person needing attention here, Dr Connor, and we have a dog.' Dr Ryde grinned at Leeton. 'And I'm a people doctor and you're a dog doctor. End of argument.' His smile deepened at the look on Leeton's face as he led Ellie away.

Ellie protested at first that she didn't need medication. Dr Ryde nodded politely, checked her arm under its dressing, clicked his tongue at burst stitches, re-titched and insisted on immediate bed. As the momentum of events slowed and reaction set in, Ellie knew Stephen was right. She took his medication to help her sleep without demur. The terrors of the last few days were still very close.

Leeton entered her room late that night. She was sharing with two other women—an electrician and a radio operator—but both women were still absent, no doubt writing letters for the ship to carry the next day. Ellie stirred to find Leeton standing over her, watching her sleep. Her eyes struggled to widen, but he put a hand on her forehead and smoothed them closed again.

'Don't even try to wake,' he said softly, bending to kiss her lightly on the forehead. 'You need your sleep.'

'So do you.' Her voice was blurred with drowsiness and love.

'I'm going now.' He touched her lips lightly with his

finger, then walked to the door. 'Sven and I have set Marbuck's leg. Once his pad is healed he'll be walking on it.'

'I'm glad.' Despite orders, her eyes opened to watch him leave.

He smiled across the room at her and his smile was a caress. 'So am I,' he said softly. 'Thank you, my Ellie.' Then he was gone, leaving her to drift where her tired mind would take her.

Dr Ryde had come early in the morning, while she was contemplating lifting her bruised body from her bunk. 'Stay there a while longer,' he ordered. 'The ship doesn't leave until noon, and you'll feel those bruises when the ship starts rolling.'

'Gee, thanks,' Ellie said ruefully.

He grinned. 'Gordon's up,' he told her. 'I've put him on crutches to go aboard the ship.' He hesitated. 'I want him thoroughly rested during the voyage, though. It's up to you to see that he is.'

She smiled. 'I can do that,' she said.

He nodded. Then he dug his hands in his pockets and stared at her, as though he was finding the next words hard to say.

'Ellie, you have to remember that for the next six weeks you too have AIDS until proven otherwise.'

She stared silently up at him.

'It's damned hard,' Stephen told her. 'Especially when there's such a small risk. But there is a risk. Unless there's a life-threatening situation on that boat you don't operate or do anything where blood transfer could occur. If someone wants you to look at their sore boil, you tell them you're a journalist and they can talk to one of the vets.'

Silence. Ellie thought back to the time she had already spent on the *Ice Maiden*. She had only been asked to advise and to dispense tablets. She could still do that.

'And another thing. . .'

She looked up at the gruff-voiced doctor beside her bunk and raised her eyebrows. It seemed the 'other thing' was also hard to say.

'I don't like the way Connor looks at you.'

Ellie raised her eyebrows even further, and Stephen gave a reluctant crack of laughter. 'I'm not a jealous lover, my dear,' he assured her. 'Believe it or not, I'm a happily married man, despite my penchant for working in absurd places. But I've seen the look in Connor's eyes when he watches you, and I don't like it.'

'You're imagining it,' Ellie said breathlessly. 'There's nothing between us.'

'Maybe there is and maybe there isn't,' Stephen said enigmatically. 'It's none of my damned business. But I'm telling you, Ellie, that whoever catches your fancy for the next six weeks, you do nothing but shake hands. When you've had the all-clear you can do whatever you like.' He grinned. 'And I hope you do.'

Ellie returned his smile, but her look was troubled. 'There's not a problem,' she said quietly, and repeated her assurance, 'there's nothing between us.'

Ellie went out on the last LARC to board the *Ice Maiden*. As they loaded the ship, the good weather of the last few days was breaking. The final loading was done with a rising wind and light snow.

Leeton was already on board. He was waiting for Ellie, reaching to help her on to the ship's deck as the men on the LARC below helped her up the ladder.

With her bags safely stowed, she returned to the deck. Leeton was waiting once again to smile his heart-wrenching smile and take her hand in his as they stood at the ship's rail. She stood silently at his side. Most of those on board were also silent, watching the last of Kellent and making their own private farewells to the Antarctic.

The last of the LARCs left the ship's side. The anchor

was lifted and the ship moved swiftly out into open water. Neither Ellie nor Leeton moved. Watching his face as Kellent disappeared from view, Ellie realised that his farewell was tinged with sadness. He loved this place.

And now he was returning to New York, to a hail of publicity and acclaim. Two years ago she would have said that such a reception was what he wanted. Now, looking at the regret in his eyes, she was not so sure.

As if sensing her eyes on him he turned to look down at her.

'How about you?' he asked gently. 'Are you sorry to leave?'

Ellie hesitated. She looked back at the bleak little settlement disappearing across the bay in the driving snow. 'I'll probably never come back,' she said frankly. 'But I'm lucky to have been here.'

'And the trauma of the last few days hasn't soured the memory?'

She shook her head. 'I'm starting to believe the Antarctic is a place we have no rights to,' she said reflectively. 'We humans have overrun every other part of the world. The Antarctic's fighting back.'

He grinned and pulled her tightly against him.

'Ouch!' she protested, but didn't pull away.

'Ditto,' he smiled. 'Just remember I've got the odd rope burn myself. Just be careful of my aching body, woman.'

'I don't think you need to worry,' Ellie said wryly.

Leeton looked around the crowded deck. The ship was packed, much more so than on Ellie's voyage down. The women were bunking together in cramped quarters, and Ellie had been told that the men were even more cramped.

'You're right, my love,' he said ruefully. 'Holding hands until Tasmania is all there is for us. But then. . .'

His eyes smiled down at her and she gasped as she

read the message in them. It was unmistakable. He wanted her.

Her eyes clouded uncertainly. Why? Was it gratitude? Was it because she was a woman and available, and his normal breed of socialite was half a world away? It didn't make sense.

Still, for now her hand lay in his and his caring warmed her. She couldn't spurn his warmth. Some things were beyond her strength. Until Tasmania, she told herself. Just for now, let me be close to him. If that's all I can ever have, then I'll take it.

The normal run for Tasmania took less than two weeks in good weather, but the *Ice Maiden* didn't strike good weather. In fact, conditions at the start of the journey were appalling.

Ellie was delighted to find she still had her sea-legs, but most weren't so lucky. Once again she found herself moving from bunk to bunk, trying to alleviate the occupant's distress.

'Marbuck's suffering too,' Leeton told her as they ate together in a near-deserted mess two days from Kellent. 'I wish I could take him on deck, but it would terrify him.'

Ellie nodded, her mind on worries of her own. Gordon was her chief concern. Seasickness was adding to his misery, and he hadn't left his bunk since they departed. Ellie wanted appropriate drugs such as AZT and she wanted specialists who were used to dealing with AIDS. She looked up to find Leeton's eyes on her. 'Problem?' he queried.

Once again there was that heart-wrenching, slow smile of his, and Ellie flushed.

'Just Gordon,' she said slowly. 'He's very seasick.'

Leeton nodded. 'He'll be all right soon,' he said confidently. 'This weather can't possibly last the whole trip. And going home must lift his depression.' He grinned. 'What Gordon needs is a loving reception back home. A ladyfriend, perhaps. . .'

Ellie forced herself to smile. For the next six weeks she was forced to be socially isolated. Hopefully then she would receive the all-clear and be free to do what she liked. For Gordon, though, the isolation was forever.

Leeton's weather prediction was correct. It was still bitterly, unseasonably cold, but the next day the ship encountered 'grease ice', thin ice lying extensively over the surface. The awful action settled to a rounded swell as the ice smoothed off the sea. Gordon was able to hold down fluid for the first time in days.

Now let's get home fast, Ellie told herself. I want him in hospital back in New York.

It was not to be. She woke the next morning to calm. She opened one eye cautiously. The world stayed horizontal. Cautiously she opened the other, expecting at any minute the sickening lurches to restart. Nothing.

Maybe I died in the night and this is what heaven feels like, she thought. The sea was calm and the ship was absolutely still. Ellie lay in the warmth of her bunk and savoured the novelty. Then she realised that there was silence added to the calm. The ship's engines had stopped.

Around her, the women in the other bunks were stirring.

'Have we hit a sand bar?'

'Sand bar? Iceberg, more like!'

'If we'd hit an iceberg we'd be in Davy Jones' locker by now.'

'Perhaps we've reached Tasmania.'

With this impossible thought the women scrambled into their clothes and headed for the deck.

They emerged to a world of dazzling white. They had been steaming through pack ice in the night. The floating ice was no longer floating. It had welded together and the *Ice Maiden* was stuck fast.

There was no water visible from the sides of the ship. Vast pressure ridges formed crazy lines across the surface of packed ice-floes. Ice-floes were jumbled and tossed like piles of dominoes thrown together, with huge slabs sloping downwards under the surface. The bow of the little ship had been forced upwards by the ice driving underneath. The *Ice Maiden* was wedged fast.

Ellie walked slowly forward to the rail, her mind numb with amazement. Leeton was already there. He turned towards her as she approached and moved aside to make room for her beside him.

'How. . .? Are we safe?' she whispered.

'Quite safe,' he assured her. His arm came around her and held her against him. 'The *Ice Maiden* is strengthened to withstand these conditions. Ships can be crushed when they're wedged between two moving ice-floes, but this is jumbled pack ice. Even if we can't get out, it'll freeze to form one piece and we'll be safe.'

Ellie nodded. 'Safe but stuck,' she said, wonderingly. 'And for how long?'

Leeton shook his head. 'Who knows? What we need is a gale to break up the ice. A strong wind combined with a high ocean swell is the only way we're going to get out of here.'

She stared at him in horror. 'And if we don't get one before this mass deepens? We're stuck for winter, aren't we?'

He shrugged. 'It's happened before,' he told her. 'The ship's equipped for just such an eventuality.'

'Can't they get us off by helicopter?'

'We're out of range of everywhere except Kellent,' Leeton said. 'And we're almost better off here than there. If we all returned to Kellent we'd just cram the place and prevent its normal winter programme going ahead. Unless the ship looks in any danger of being crushed, I'll guess we'll stay exactly where we are.'

He smiled reasssuringly at her worried face. 'I guess

for us it's no big deal,' he told her. 'By the time we get home our combined articles are going to be fantastic.'

'I don't. . . I don't think. . .' Ellie's eyes had filled with horror. Flooding her mind was the thought of Gordon. Six months without AZT. . .without doctors who knew how to treat him. . . He'd be dead well within that time.

'What's wrong?' Leeton was watching her closely.

She shook her head, turning aside to go below. It was better she break the news to Gordon than anyone else. But Leeton was grasping her by the wrist.

'Why the tragedy?' he demanded, his voice suddenly harsh. 'There are many on board with a far greater need to be home than you.'

Ellie gazed at him hopelessly. She couldn't tell him. She had made that promise to Gordon and she had to keep it.

'Walter wants those articles,' she said weakly. 'The magazine's depending on them. . .' She pulled her wrist from his grasp and turned away.

The hoped-for bad weather didn't come. Day after day dawned cold but calm, cementing the little ship firmly into its icy base.

Five hundred yards from the *Ice Maiden* was open water. Passengers and crew took turns digging to free the ship from the ice wedged against the bow. With a clear path to gain speed, the *Ice Maiden* might ram her way free.

It took days of labour to break through twenty feet of ice, then, for a day, the ship was shunted back and forth in the cleared channel. It got nowhere. Finally night fell, and in the morning the channel had refrozen.

Ellie had helped dig, but much of her free time had been spent with Gordon. Seated on deck, rugged up against the icy wind, he had watched the proceedings with hopeless eyes. He knew as well as Ellie that failure to free the ship was his death sentence.

As the captain gave the order to cease trying and it was clear there was no hope of freedom, Gordon said nothing. He picked up his crutches and went below. Ellie watched him go with fearful eyes. Then she went down to the privacy of her bunk and wept.

At dinner that evening it was obvious she had been weeping. Leeton watched her enter the mess and seat herself as far from him as possible. His eyes grew cold and hard, and for the first time since they'd come on board he did not come near her. Finally, as coffee was served, he stood and walked over to her table.

'Tears, Dr Michaels?'

Ellie looked up at him helplessly. It was no use denying her distress. She had been stupid to weep — stupid and unprofessional. She couldn't help it, though. Gordon had become a friend, and she knew what he was facing.

'I am upset,' she said wearily.

He stood looking down at her bowed head, his face creased in incomprehension. 'Why?' he asked harshly. He gestured around him. 'Pete over there hasn't seen his brand-new son yet. And Connie was due to be married last week. Her fiancé flew to Tasmania early to meet the boat and as far as she knows is still sitting on the wharf. But they're not crying, Dr Michaels. So what makes it such a tragedy for you?'

Around them people were turning their heads to stare, and Ellie cringed under their gaze. She shouldn't have come to the mess. She couldn't defend herself.

It wouldn't be long, she thought sadly. It wouldn't be long before Gordon became so ill that it would be impossible to keep his diagnosis from the rest of the ship. And if she had to endure Leeton's coldness and the disdain of her fellow passengers until that time, then it was a small pain compared to what Gordon must endure.

Her mind told her that, but it didn't stop the hurt as Leeton's cold eyes brushed over her. She stood up, the tears coming afresh in her eyes.

'Perhaps it's the thought of being stuck in a ship for six months with you,' she said savagely.

After weeks stuck in the ice, life began to assume a rhythm. Research projects were started and the ship began to hum with activity.

Once the ice was firm around the ship the ice became an expanded recreation area. A soccer field was marked out and soon everyone was being drawn into the increasingly competitve games.

Apart from Leeton, her distress didn't seem to have alienated many others. To her dismay, Ellie found she was constantly used as the ship's doctor. For the short trip to Tasmania she had anticipated no need for her services. Now, however, as the occupants of the ship were out on the ice engaged in their various projects and the energetic soccer matches, she found she was in demand for everything from sprained ankles to frostbite.

She coped by gloving for everything, to the point where she was teased for her excessive care.

'It's New York training,' she told them. 'I've been trained to glove and gown to prescribe antibiotics from a hundred paces.'

Leeton watched her remove a sliver of wood from one of the crew members' hands and raised his brows as well at her double gloving. 'Some precautions,' he said ironically. 'What is it exactly you're afraid of catching?'

Ellie flushed but said nothing. She wondered what his reaction would be if he knew she was afraid of exactly the opposite.

The air between her and Leeton stayed icy. It was as if he regretted ever allowing any warmth to enter their relationship. He was more than making up for it now, Ellie thought sadly. His comments to her were confined to stinging barbs, or, when she was present, conversations with others such as Sven on their need to be at home. Sven had hoped desperately to be home in time for his daughter's third birthday.

Finally Ellie learned to live with the coolness. Perhaps it was just as well, she thought sadly. She had no strength to hold him at arm's length, and to see him every day on the ship was an agony in itself. It was impossible to avoid him in the cramped confines of the ship. Every corner she turned he seemed to be there, watching her with sardonic eyes.

'Learning to accept your prison with good grace?' Leeton quizzed her mockingly three weeks after their enforced halt. He had come up behind her as she watched one of the ship's interminable soccer games. The soccer was at best amateurish, and considerably marred by Marbuck's unshakeable conviction that the ball was being kicked for his benefit.

Ellie shook her head and said nothing, then looked up thankfully as Sven joined them. One of the players came off and Leeton was dragged on to take his place. Sven and Ellie stood side by side and watched as Leeton turned into a soccer player. Lean and skilled, with his athletic prowess he more than made up for his lack of familiarity with the game.

Sven stood easily beside her. They had become good friends. On the ground, Leeton had possession of the ball and was guiding it skilfully through the ranks of his opponents. Ellie's eyes followed him, unaware that Sven was watching her.

'You and Leeton—there is iciness between you that has nothing to do with the temperature.' Sven's eyes gently quizzed her, and Ellie flushed. 'You love him, don't you?' Sven went on conversationally, as if it had been something he had been meaning to ask her for some time.

She looked swiftly over at him, in shock. Sven's eyes were kind but appraising. She flushed again and stared at the ground.

Sven nodded thoughtfully as if Ellie had just confirmed his suspicions in words.

'And he you?'

On the ice Leeton had his opponents in disarray. He was moving fast, searching for an opportunity to shoot for goal. Ellie laughed without humour. 'Don't be funny,' she said bitterly. 'What would the great Leeton Connor want with someone like me?'

Sven's head tilted and he said nothing. Out on the field Leeton's team scored triumphantly despite a noisy protest from the opposition.

'I have to go,' Ellie said stiffly. 'I need to dress Gordon's leg.'

'It's not getting better quickly.'

'It's a bite,' she told him. 'And bites are notoriously slow to heal. There's been some infection. . .'

Sven nodded. He turned away to accompany her to the ladder leading up to the ship. As he stood aside to let her lead he laid a restraining hand on her shoulder.

'Ellie, you could give a lot to Leeton,' he said quietly. 'Don't put yourself down in deference to Leeton's other life. He's had a lot of women in his time, but, as far as I know, none like you. And, for all he's been the object of every society hopeful since he was eighteen, he's never married any of them.'

Ellie stared at Sven's kindly, concerned face and turned to climb the ladder. 'I don't see that I have much choice,' she said bitterly. 'He doesn't want me.'

Sven came to find her the following morning. He was armed with maps, rucksacks and cross-country skis, and his eyes were alight with enthusiasm.

'There's a king penguin rookery just along the coast from here,' he announced. 'It was sighted five years ago, but as far as I know no human has ever been there. According to my map we must be no further than three miles from there. The ice is rock-solid from here to the shore, the weather is good, so I think we should try.'

Ellie looked up from her morning coffee-cup and smiled at his enthusiasm.

'Come on,' he told her. 'Once the winter sets in we are stuck on the ship for months. We should make the most of the good weather.'

She hesitated. The temptation to be away from the ship and her tensions with Leeton was irresistible. She smiled up at the big, bearded Swede and rose.

'Lovely. What are you doing with the penguins?'

'Counting them,' he said. 'If I can get a rough idea of how many there are it will be useful.'

For what, Ellie didn't know. She didn't need to ask. It was enough that she was going.

She prepared carefully. Ready, she climbed down the ladder to find Sven discussing their route with the ship's captain. Leeton stood beside them, and he too was dressed to go.

'L-Leeton' Ellie stammered.

He looked up, his eyes cool. 'Dr Michaels. I didn't know we were having the pleasure of your company.'

Sven turned to them and smiled. 'We can count faster and more accurately with three,' he said briefly. 'I hope you can ski, Ellie?'

'I can.' Her voice was terse. She had the feeling she was being manipulated.

'Let's go, then,' Sven ordered.

The ski-run was glorious. For Ellie it was the first physical exertion she had had in weeks. The pack ice had been smoothed by frozen snow over the time they had been trapped, and was now a perfect surface for skiing. Ellie put Leeton from her mind, put her head down and raced.

She was aware of the men beside her, but only just. Leeton was keeping pace with her and she felt his rhythm matching hers. It felt good. She was as one with the skis, and the day was magnificent.

She was hardly aware when Sven dropped behind. His skiing had been perfect, but all of a sudden he wasn't there. A shout from behind brought her to a standstill.

She turned to find him crouched in the snow, with Leeton bending over him in concern. Swiftly she skied back to the two men.

'I've turned my ankle.' Sven swore softly. 'Never do I do such a thing on open ground. I must have been air-dreaming.'

Ellie frowned. 'Loosen your boot,' she ordered.

Sven shook his head. 'No,' he told her. 'If I do it will not go back on.'

'OK.' Leeton's voice was clipped and authoritative. 'Can you bear weight?'

Sven stood up and gingerly stepped on his foot. His face cleared. 'It is all right,' he smiled. 'Just twisted. But I am afraid I must return to the ship.'

'We all return to the ship,' Leeton said.

'Nonsense.' Sven looked back the way they had come. Across the plateau of white was a tiny speck in the distance that was the *Ice Maiden*. 'I can see the ship from here. There is no trouble I can get into. The penguins need to be counted, and you two can do it for me.'

'But not by ourselves.' There was no mistaking the dismay in Ellie's voice, and Sven smiled down at her.

'But yes,' he said. 'By yourselves.'

He would brook no argument. To do anything else was staring a perfect opportunity in the face, he said, and if anyone else but Leeton Connor had been beside her Ellie would have agreed.

Finally they watched him ski off back towards the ship. Ellie's eyes narrowed with sudden suspicion as she watched him go. Surely a man with a twisted ankle couldn't move so fast. . .

She turned back to find Leeton watching with an expression of equal suspicion on his face. He looked down at her and his face broke into a reluctant grin. 'Do you have the feeling we've been set up?' he demanded, and she had to smile.

'All right,' he continued, 'let's get these damned penguins counted and get back to the ship. I only hope the rookery wasn't a figment of Sven's imagination.'

It wasn't. Two miles further on they found it. The unmistakable smell and noise attracted them as they neared the shoreline, and Ellie stared in awe at the hundreds of three-quarter-grown penguins. They were bigger than the adelies, and the few adult birds seemed much more. . . She searched for the word. Regal, she decided. More like kings. . .

Counting them was a logistical nightmare, but Leeton guided her through the procedure with ease.

'It's impossible to be accurate,' he told her. 'We simply grid the area, mark off densities and then do random counts of low, medium and high density squares. We do it three times each and average the results, giving high and low estimates for error factors. And only count chicks. We can estimate parent bird numbers from chick numbers.'

Ellie nodded. In full efficiency she could ignore the fact that it was Leeton standing beside her, Leeton who was issuing orders and Leeton who was the only other person for three lonely miles.

Finally the counting was done. Leeton swung the rucksack from his back and carried it away from the noisy rookery.

'Lunch,' he ordered.

Ellie was using her camera almost as a shield. She

took some biscuits and cheese and moved away, still photographing.

'I'm not about to attack you, Dr Michaels.' Leeton's voice was laced with sarcasm, and she winced. Finally she met his look. Leeton stared at her for a long moment, then packed up the remaining lunch. 'Sven's gone to a great deal of trouble to make this little tête-à-tête possible,' he said quietly. 'The least we can do is to oblige him by talking.'

Ellie didn't answer.

'Why do you want to go home?' he flung at her.

'Everyone on the ship wants to go home,' she said sullenly. 'I'm not the only one.'

He shook his head. 'You're more upset than Sven. And I want to know why.'

She took a deep breath. 'Walter wants these articles,' she said stiffly. 'And they're good.'

He nodded. 'So personal glory is waiting for you in New York. . .'

'That's not fair.'

He raised his eyebrows. 'Isn't it?'

Silence. Suddenly Leeton threw his rucksack on to the ice and came towards her. 'What the hell is going on?' he demanded suddenly. 'Do you know how close I came to convincing myself I was in love with you?'

Ellie took a ragged intake of breath. 'That's. . .that's crazy,' she gasped.

'Isn't it?' he mocked. His hands gripped her shoulders and held. 'I spend two years thinking you a muck-raking bitch and then you risk your silly little neck for my friend and again for my dog. . . Is that "personal glory" stuff too, Ellie?'

She met his look with pain-filled eyes. 'That's right,' she whispered. 'I pulled Marbuck up for the honour and glory associated with it. I only hope I get to feature on the front page of the *Daily*.'

Leeton's grip was hurting her. Around them a group

of penguin chicks were staring in interest at their unusual visitors. Ellie was oblivious. She was oblivious to everything except Leeton.

He shook his head. 'It doesn't make sense,' he said. 'You don't make sense. And the way I feel doesn't make sense either.' And he pulled her to him and kissed her closed mouth.

Ellie froze. Her whole heart was responding to him. He was all she wanted. All she ever needed in life was to be held by this man, to be kissed by this man. And she couldn't. Not now. . . Not yet. . .

Stephen Ryde's words came screaming back at her. 'You too have AIDS until proven otherwise.' And if she did. . . If, by letting Leeton kiss her, she was exposing the man she loved to risk—for it was obvious that he wanted more. . .

Her body was rigid under his grasp. His searching lips met nothing but hard rejection. She gave a moàn of pain and pushed away.

'No!'

He let her go. Standing back, he stared at her with blank, uncomprehending eyes. 'Ellie. . .' His voice was shaken. For once, the great Leeton Connor was unsure.

'Leave me alone,' she said desperately. 'I don't want this.'

He shook his head. 'You mean you don't feel what I'm feeling?'

Never before had Ellie come so close to breaking a promise. It would be so easy. To tell Leeton all that she was feeling, to fling herself on his chest, to feel his arms comfort and caress her. . .

She couldn't. It was not her secret to impart. It was Gordon who had to matter. And Gordon who had asked her not to tell. . .

'No,' she said flatly, her eyes reflecting blank despair.

'I don't believe you.' He reached for her and she stepped back, fighting for words to drive him from her.

He couldn't come close. He couldn't. . . She couldn't bear it.

'Well, you have to,' she spat at him. 'You threatened to rape me once before, and you have me alone again. I can't stop you touching me, but I'd rather kiss a fish! I don't want you, Leeton Connor. So don't come near me!' Her voice was very nearly a yell, and she stopped, her breath caught on a sob. She turned away and bent to pull on her skis.

The silence stretched out. Ellie didn't look up—she couldn't. If she did she would break entirely. When Leeton finally spoke his voice seemed to come from a long way away.

'Very well, Dr Michaels. Message received. If that's the way you want it, that's the way it will be.'

The journey back to the ship was done in silence. Ellie fought back tears all the way, agonisingly conscious of the man beside her. What he was thinking she couldn't begin to guess. It seemed he was destined to loathe her forever. A spoiled little bitch for whom he had felt a momentary physical attraction. . .nothing more.

Sven was watching for them as they returned. One look at their faces told him that his scheming had not paid off.

'You're not limping,' Ellie snapped at him as he helped carry her skis to the store-room.

'I heal fast.' He smiled ruefully. 'I had hoped my ankle might have achieved something.'

'Well, it didn't,' she said waspishly. She sighed, then, as she met Sven's worried gaze, gave a rueful smile. 'I'm sorry, Sven. Thank you for trying. But I told you— some things just aren't meant to be.'

An hour later Ellie emerged from her bunk feeling a little more composed. Not much, but a little. The sounds of raised voices made her go up to investigate.

The whole complement of passengers and crew were, it seemed, on the deck. Gordon saw Ellie emerge from the hatchway. His pale face was eager as he limped towards her.

'We're expecting company,' he told her. He pointed towards the horizon. Where the sky met the sea was a low red shape — another ship.

'It's one of the giant Japanese ice-breakers,' Gordon told her excitedly. 'They made radio contact half an hour ago. They're going to try and break us out of here.'

The jubilation on the deck lasted for more than an hour. By nightfall, however, the exultation was dimming. The huge ship ploughed towards them, throwing up vast slabs of ice, but as it reached within a few hundred yards of the *Ice Maiden* it slowed and stopped. Around the *Ice Maiden* the ice thickened to become an almost impenetrable slab. Even the huge newcomer was having trouble.

Ellie stayed on deck while her fingers and hands slowly numbed, watching the ship trying to reach them. For the ice-breaker itself the slab wasn't a problem. It seemed to simply run over the top. The *Ice Maiden* however, had to have a clear channel.

As darkness covered the scene, the group of watchers on the *Ice Maiden* fell silent. The Japanese ship was making no headway at all. Leeton came up to where Ellie was standing at the rail.

'It seems you might be staying on after all,' he said savagely. 'The world can wait a little longer for Dr Ellie Michaels' scoop.'

Ellie flushed. Beside her, Gordon silently left the rail and turned to go below. She followed him with her eyes, and Leeton's hurtful words washed over her.

'That will please you, I think,' she said quietly, then brushed past Leeton and followed Gordon.

*   *   *

With the morning came a decision. The ice-breaker was making no headway and could not risk staying where it was. The longer it stayed, the stronger the risk that it too would be trapped. Before it left, though, it sent a message saying it could accommodate twenty extra passengers. They had to be ready to leave in an hour.

The news flew around the *Ice Maiden* in a breathless hush. The men with families back home found hope flaring within. Only twenty, though. . .

The captain, a big, gruff man in his sixties, assembled both crew and passengers on the deck.

'Decide for yourselves,' he told them. 'There's a lot of you with damned good reasons to go home. If you think your reason justifies your being in the twenty, come and tell me in the next fifteen minutes. Then I'll make a decision. I'll post a list of twenty names, and that list is final.' He turned and stomped below, clearly not relishing the task before him.

'Going to submit the story of a lifetime as a reason?' Leeton's voice was quietly mocking in her ear. 'This is your big chance, Ellie.'

Ellie flushed and moved away. She needed to find Gordon.

'We have to tell,' she told him a few minutes later. 'Gordon, as far as the captain knows, you have a healing leg. That won't guarantee you a place.'

Gordon shook his head. 'I don't want to take someone else's place,' he said quietly.

'You'll die if you don't,' she told him, her voice blunt. 'No one has a better reason. I have to tell the captain.'

'OK, Ellie.'

Half an hour later Ellie was standing for the second time in front of Captain Larsen. She had outlined the facts twenty minutes before and watched the captain's face drop with incredulity.

'Of course he has to go,' the captain had agreed. 'But I have to tell the Japanese captain that he has AIDS.'

'Must you?'

'I must,' the captain had told her.

Now, ten minutes later, Ellie had been called back. The captain was looking grim.

'Won't they take him?' she asked fearfully. She had been afraid of as much.

The captain shook his head. 'They will,' he told her. 'But they're insisting on you too. No doctor, no AIDS patient — as simple as that.'

'But he doesn't need me. . .'

'If they get stuck themselves he will need you, and they haven't a doctor on board,' the captain told her. 'I'm sorry, Dr Michaels, as much as I'd like to keep our only doctor and give your berth to another person, I'm afraid you're going. So pack — now!'

Ellie made her way to her cabin without looking to right or left. All around, there were people discussing who would get to board the Japanese ship. Ellie received some curious glances as she passed, but her mind was numb. All these people wanting to go home and she, Ellie, was to take the place of one of them.

She briefly looked in on Gordon. 'Pack,' she told him. 'You're on the list.' He opened his mouth to comment, but she was already gone. She didn't want to tell Gordon the conditions of his going. Time enough for him to find out as they boarded. For now the guilt was only hers.

She packed swiftly and then sat on the bunk, waiting for the sound of the small helicopter based on the Japanese vessel which would be used for the transfer. Leeton found her there.

'So it was true.' He entered swiftly but stopped as he saw the pile of duffel bags waiting to go. His steel-grey eyes were expressionless. He stood by the door and waited for her to talk.

'It's true,' Ellie said.

There was a long-drawn-out silence. Then Leeton nodded slowly, as if it was something he should have expected.

'Did you know Sven's name is not on the list?' he asked, with silk-smooth courtesy. 'Gordon made it, because of his leg and general ill health, but not Sven. For some reason Dr Michaels' reason for returning home is more imperative than Sven's need to see his little girls.'

Ellie bit her lip and said nothing. She couldn't.

'What did you tell the captain, Ellie?' Leeton asked softly, savagely. 'What lies did you tell him? Or is it money from the other end that's doing it? Is *Our Planet's Health* somehow greasing palms to get its precious Antarctic story?'

'That's not true,' Ellie said desperately, and Leeton laughed in disbelief.

'Isn't it?' he asked bitterly. 'I seem to remember you swallowed your principles once before in writing a sensational story. How much more of a scoop is this? An ice-bound ship and you have pictures coming out of your ears. You'll have a world scoop, and you know it.'

'Isn't that what you want?' Ellie whispered. 'Publicity for your precious Antarctic?'

'Not at the cost of my integrity,' he said harshly.

'Leeton. . .' Her hands went out in a futile entreaty. There were no words to back it up. The hands dropped again and she buried her face. 'Please, Lee. . .'

'Don't do it, Ellie.' His eyes were hard and unyielding. Then, at the sight of her slumped figure, they suddenly softened and he put out a finger to touch her hair. 'Ellie, I keep hoping I'm mistaken in you. I keep hoping that the image I've been carrying of you for two years was a nonsense. Please don't do this. . .'

She shook her head. She pulled her hands away from her eyes and met his. 'I must,' she said quietly.

In the distance there was the sound of a helicopter.

Ellie took a deep breath and stooped to pick up her bags. 'Let me go, Dr Connor,' she said. 'My name is on the list. I have the right.'

'You selfish little. . .' Leeton shook his head in disbelief. 'You'll live to regret this,' he warned. 'You and your precious magazine. . .'

'Don't threaten me,' Ellie said quietly. She moved deliberately to the door. 'Leeton, I have to go.'

He moved aside to let her past. That was her last sight of him, a lean and angry man, his whole being rejecting utterly both her and her actions.

As she moved to the upper deck to board the helicopter Ellie met Sven. He looked at her, then away. He didn't say a word. The image of pain clearly etched on his face stayed with her as she boarded the helicopter and started her long journey home.

Two weeks later Ellie assisted Gordon from the plane at New York. Her time in the Antarctic was over.

CHAPTER ELEVEN

THE *Ice Maiden* broke free from the ice seven months later, and when it did Ellie was no longer working for *Our Planet's Health*. She would return at some indefinite time in the future, but for now she was living in a big rambling house on Long Island, waiting for Gordon to die.

There were no regrets at what she had done. To her relief, Gordon had responded well to the AZT. He had had five healthy months, months when he had assisted her in writing her articles and watched them come into print to national and international acclaim. His algae research had received more coverage than he had dared hope for — one of Ellie's photographs taken the day of the leopard seal attack appeared on the front cover of *Our Planet's Health* and was reprinted in papers all over the world — and even his skuas received attention.

'I feel I've done something worthwhile,' he had told Ellie the last time he came into her office. 'I may have a damnable disease that's going to cut me off short, but at least I've done something.' He had picked up the last issue of her magazine and smiled. 'You don't know how good that feels, and it's thanks to you.'

She had smiled up at him, unable to suppress a niggle of anxiety at his gaunt face. AIDS was inexorable, she thought sadly, thanking the powers that be for the thousandth time that the results of her tests had all proved negative. Whether she would have had Gordon's courage she wasn't sure. She was only grateful she didn't have to find out.

They had worked on one last article together, and the next time Ellie heard from him was indirectly. His mother had contacted her to let her know that he was dying.

The elderly lady had burst into tears on the phone. 'They've taken him to hospital,' she said. 'We so wanted to keep him at home, but the girls are all married and flown, and George and I can't nurse him on our own.'

Her words had stayed with Ellie, haunting her. The next day she had told Walter she was taking extended leave, packed her bags and taken up residence in the home of Gordon's parents. Gordon had been brought home the next day.

It was hard work. Gordon was nearing the last stages of his disease, and was dependent on her for everything. 'Ellie, I'll never be able to thank you,' he had whispered to her as she had administered morphine in the small hours of a long, pain-racked night. 'If I were fabulously wealthy I'd leave you my fortune. But there's nothing.'

'But your friendship,' Ellie had told him, gripping his weak hand on the coverlet. 'And that's enough. Besides,' she had smiled, 'I'm a journalist who desperately wants to go back to being a doctor. This way I'm both. Your parents have set me up a wonderful desk on the porch overlooking the ocean, and I'm writing some of the best freelance articles I've ever done.'

It was true. The sadness and emotion of the past twelve months had added depth and maturity to her writing. Walter read her work with satisfaction. It was almost worth losing his star reporter from his immediate staff for a while.

Ellie read of the release of the *Ice Maiden* with a curious, detached interest. She knew Leeton would still carry anger towards her, but she needn't see him. Leeton was a part of her that had been cut away with her action on the ship. There was nothing left. It was gone. She loved him — it was a part of her that nothing could alter — but there was no love that could ever come to her. Her relationship with Leeton Connor was finished.

She forgot that he would want to see Gordon.

He arrived one bleak December day when Gordon was desperately ill. Ellie had sat up all the previous night, waiting for the end. Gordon's eldest sister arrived in the morning and relieved her for a while, but she had dissolved into tears and had ended up having to be comforted and cared for herself. Ellie had taken up her vigil again, trying to make Gordon as comfortable as she could.

The doorbell's peal through the house didn't disturb her; for the last few days Gordon's parents had suffered a constant flow of curious and sympathetic relations. Ellie tried to fend them off, but this afternoon she was too tired. Mrs Fraser or Gordon's sister would just have to cope. Then the door opened and Leeton Connor appeared.

Neither spoke. Ellie was seated on the far side of the bed, watching the intravenous drip flow slowly into Gordon's veins. She must be asleep, she thought wearily — asleep and dreaming. She shook her head as if trying to clear the fog, and Leeton entered, closing the door behind him.

He hadn't known. One look at his shocked face told Ellie that he had expected to find Gordon healthy and welcoming. Instead. . . Her fingers automatically reached for Gordon's pulse. He was still with them, but only just.

'My God.' Leeton stared down at his friend and then across at Ellie. 'What. . .?'

'AIDS,' Ellie said softly. There could be no keeping it from him now.

He said nothing, but his eyes said it all. The shock, the horror and finally the absolute comprehension. Then, as he opened his mouth to speak, Gordon's mother opened the door and came into the room.

'Dr Connor,' she said softly, casting an anxious glance down at her unconscious son. 'Julie — Gordon's sister — told me you'd come. But I'm sorry. . .' Her voice faltered a little. 'She didn't realise you wouldn't know. She said you rang this morning to see if Gordon was home, and she assumed you were just asking whether he was home from hospital. And then when you arrived and asked to see him she just showed you in. . .' The elderly lady paused, her distress obvious. 'You're our son's friend,' she said falteringly. 'We wouldn't have had you find out like this. . .'

Leeton crossed to her and put a hand on her shoulder. 'There's no easy way to hear news like this,' he told her gently. Then he too turned to look at his friend. 'How long?' he asked.

Ellie shrugged. 'He hasn't been conscious for the last three days,' she told him. 'It's very close.'

'Dr Michaels brought him home from hospital,' Mrs Fraser said tremulously. 'She's been here all the time. If it hadn't been for her ——' She broke off, tears sliding down her wrinkled cheeks. Then she took Leeton's hands in hers. 'Gordon's father would like to see you,' she said. 'He's. . .he only comes in here when he's by himself. He's not coping all that well.'

'I'd say you were all coping,' Leeton said firmly. His eyes met Ellie's across the bed, and she read his stunned incomprehension. 'I'd say you were coping magnificently.' He crossed to the bed and looked down at the sleeping face of his friend. Wordlessly he picked up the gaunt hand that Ellie had just laid on the coverlet, held it for a long moment and then turned to allow Mrs Fraser to usher him out of the room.

Two days later Gordon died. Ellie was revolving in a weary world of sadness. She attended to her patient and had time for little else.

Professional detachment? she thought humourlessly

as she sat by Gordon on the last night. Where was it? Not here. She had become so involved in this close family's grief that it was as if she was one of them.

They also felt it. 'Stay on,' Mrs Fraser told her. 'At least until the funeral.' But Ellie shook her head. Her place wasn't here.

The funeral was huge. Ellie went to the church and stood in the grounds watching the vast number of people making their way in. Almost the entire Antarctic contingent was there. She saw Sven with his wife beside him, and there was Leeton. . .

She had seen his photograph splashed on the newsstands that morning, and cameramen were at the entrance to the church. He would have been inundated by the Press since he had returned. He waved the cameramen impatiently aside, then cast a quick glance around the church grounds before entering. He didn't see Ellie, and she didn't wish him to.

She couldn't go in. She had meant to—had dressed and come especially—but it seemed all wrong, to go into this place to say goodbye to a friend for whom she had said all the goodbyes she could ever say. The Frasers would understand, she knew. Her place wasn't here. Besides, she couldn't face Leeton. . .

She waited until the church was full and the organ blared forth its solemn tone. Then she turned and left.

The following Monday she walked back into the offices of *Our Planet's Health*. Walter was expecting her. He rose from behind his desk, and the normally undemonstrative man crossed to envelop her in a massive hug. Then he held her at arm's length.

'You look as if you've been through a wringer,' he told her.

'Thanks,' she said wryly. 'That's just what a girl wants to hear.'

He grinned, but his eyes were sympathetic. 'I wasn't expecting you back so soon,' he told her. 'I was surprised when you rang last week and said you were returning.'

'I want to work,' she told him definitely. It was all she could think of to do. In leisure there was only heartache and loneliness.

Walter nodded slowly. 'What you need is some sun,' he told her. 'And I have just the assignment for you. If you must work, at least I can get you away from New York's winter.'

Ellie's heart sank. 'Not the Sahara again?' she said cautiously. 'I think I'd rather face the ice of the Antarctic than all that sand.'

Walter shook his head. 'No,' he told her. 'Something much more civilised.' He handed her an itinerary and stood back, watching her face as she read it.

'Norfolk Island?' she said in bewilderment. 'Why on earth would I want to go to Norfolk Island?'

'To interview Professor David Einfield,' Walter told her. 'Have you heard of him?'

'He's at Stanford,' Ellie said slowly. 'Working on the ageing process. Rumour has it that he has some new development in the pipeline that slows ageing by as much as a half. But he doesn't give interviews. . .'

'. . .while he's working,' Walter finished triumphantly. 'But he's agreed to give us one while he's on vacation. Full-length — as in-depth as we want. His only stipulation is that we send someone who knows what he's talking about.'

'But. . .'

'No buts,' Walter said firmly. 'There's a flight this evening. I want you on it.'

'But Walter. . .'

'Ellie, I want you back working full-time or not at all,' Walter snapped, suddenly grim. 'I know your friend's death has upset you. If you don't want to work, say so and take a holiday. But if you're back at work then you're doing this interview.'

Ellie hesitated. The last thing she wanted was a holiday, with time to think. She desperately had to be busy. Finally she spread her hands in a gesture of defeat. 'OK,' she said.

'Good.' Walter smiled, affability itself now he had his way. 'Don't forget to pack a bikini. And take your time getting a really good report. The ramifications of the professor's work are enormous.'

Ellie nodded. Her mind was racing. Leeton, it was saying over and over again. What if he wants to see you? You won't be here.

He won't, she told herself. He'll be back with his friends, surrounded by his social set. He won't have time for me.

'You haven't had any feedback from Dr Connor?' she asked slowly. 'About my articles, I mean.'

'I have, as a matter of fact,' Walter beamed at her. 'He came in on Friday. Congratulations all round. And he asked me to pass his personal thanks to you.'

Friday — the day after the funeral. . . Ellie took a deep breath. 'I'm sorry I missed him.'

'Frank will do a follow-up interview in six months,' Walter said. 'We won't get near him for a while now. He's hot news.' He glanced at his watch. 'Enough, though, Ellie. The Antarctic is last week's news. This week is Professor Einfield. And you have packing to do and a plane to catch.' He placed plane tickets and an itinerary in one of her hands and a sheaf of papers in the other. 'Do your homework on the way,' he ordered.

By the time Ellie landed on Norfolk she was thoroughly disorientated. Too much had happened too fast. She sat on the plane and stared at Professor Einfield's notes, but they made not one word of sense.

I'm going to have to get my head in order before I meet the man, she thought. But for now, all she could think of was her overwhelming sense of loss. Leeton was back in the States and she was here. What she had hoped for she didn't admit, even to herself, but whatever it was it hadn't happened. What lay before her was work and more work.

Even the beauty of Norfolk could not dim the pain in her heart. The small plane that had linked with her flight to Sydney circled twice before landing, enabling her to see the vast cliffs, the deep swell of the Pacific Ocean and the magnificent, undulating grazing land below. The island was dotted with towering Norfolk pines. They seemed so tall that they added height to the small island, making the slashes of cliff-face rise to majestic heights.

A battered taxi took her from the airport to her hotel. It drove slowly, stopping every now and then to let a cow wander across the road.

'The cows have right of way around here,' the taxi driver explained. 'You hit one, you pay. Plus,' he grinned, 'you bury the cow!'

Ellie's hotel was a tiny guest-house nestled in overgrown, subtropical gardens on a headland overlooking the ocean. The owner showed her to her room with obvious pride.

'This is the best room,' he told her. 'The travel agent said you were to have the best, and this is it.'

She frowned. The room was fabulous, luxuriously appointed with every conceivable comfort. Vast French windows opened out to a balcony overlooking the sea. Stairs dropped down to a track meandering invitingly into the gardens, obviously leading down to the blue-green rock pools below the house.

It was a stunning room. What was Walter thinking of, to provide his staff with such luxuries? She thought back to some of the dingy, third-rate hotels she had stayed in on past assignments, and shook her head in disbelief.

'Is Professor Einfield in?' she asked the owner. The

notes Walter had given her said the professor would be staying in the same hotel.

The man shook his head. 'He and his wife are out walking. They walk most days. They'll be back for dinner, maybe.' He shrugged. 'And I only run to three rooms. Exclusive is what we are. There's only you and the Einfields and Dr Connor. . .'

'Dr Connor!'

'Mm.' The man beamed at her. 'Nice chap — famous, they say. Even been in the papers here. You might have read about him. He's been stuck on that ship in the Antarctic.'

'I know.' Ellie's world was whirling. She stared down at her suitcases, overwhelmed by the compulsion to pick them up and run. What on earth. . .?

'Hello, Ellie.'

He was there, standing in the doorway, his slow smile enveloping her and his eyes a caress. Ellie's breath caught in her throat. She didn't move — she couldn't.

'You folks know each other?' Their host was beaming from Ellie to Leeton. 'Well, now, that's great.' He picked up Ellie's cases and carried them over to the storage cupboard. 'I'll leave you to it, then,' he smiled. 'See you at dinner.'

He reached the door, cast another look at Leeton and hesitated. 'That is unless you want to eat alone?' he ventured. 'We do a lovely private dinner on the balcony. Mostly for honeymooners, but. . .' he looked at Leeton's face. '. . .sometimes for folks who feel about the same.' He retired, chuckling.

Ellie's face was turning from crimson to ashen white and back to crimson. She put her hands up to her burning cheeks, trying to drive away the colour. 'What . . .what are you doing here?' she whispered.

'Waiting for you.'

She was close to tears. 'I don't understand.' It was a

plaintive whisper. Leeton's smile deepened and he crossed the room to take her hands into his.

'You needed a holiday,' he said. 'A fool could see that. And after two years of the Antarctic, a skiing holiday in the French Alps didn't really appeal. So here we are.'

'But Professor Einfield. . .'

'My good friend David,' Leeton smiled. 'You'll meet him later on. He holidays here every year, and he's happy to give you all the interviews you require.' His smile deepened. 'He's here for a month, though, Ellie. And I warned Walter that he's a very slow man to interview.'

'Walter knew. . .'

Leeton nodded gravely. 'Walter knew. I think the idea of playing Cupid appealed.'

Ellie gave a little sob of pure emotion. She looked up at Leeton and the look in his eyes made her heart twist into a knot of desire and of love. She pulled back, shaking.

'And you. . .'

'You're exhausted,' he said slowly. He put a hand up to touch the dark shadows under her eyes. 'Two days' plane travel on top of last week. . .' He smiled. 'I want you to sleep,' he ordered. 'And later we'll have that private dinner our host so rashly promised.' He bent, kissed her lightly on the cheek and left her to her wonder.

To her surprise Ellie did sleep. She didn't think she ever could, but the soft white linen of the bed beckoned. She placed her head on the pillow for a moment and woke four hours later.

She woke to a cloud of absolute joy. It was all around her, enveloping her in a mist of pure happiness.

'Don't be silly,' she told herself aloud. 'He's indulging me because of what I did for Gordon.'

He wouldn't look at me like that if that was all it was, an inner voice retorted. The joy would not recede. It bubbled up and over as she showered and changed into a soft silk dress for dinner.

He's only seen me in jeans and working clothes, she thought as she unpacked her suitcase. She had brought formal clothes, however, not knowing what sort of man Professor Einfield might be. If he had wanted formal interviews over formal meals she had been prepared.

So she pulled on a soft white dress of handmade silk with strapless top and clinging skirt. She had bought it years before when she had dressed for Sam, but Sam had never liked this. Virginal, he had called it, mocking, and made her change into something more sophisticated. It hadn't mattered that she had loved it.

The shadows under her eyes had not faded and could not be hidden by make-up. They made her wide brown eyes seem enormous. 'You look fourteen,' she told herself. But she knew she didn't. Not in this dress, which clung to her figure so revealingly and showed the smooth curves of her full, rounded breasts. She brushed her soft brown hair until it shone, banishing the thought from her mind that she was doing it for Leeton.

She cast one long look at herself in the long mirror and shook her head. She was crazy, she thought, fighting the desire to retire to jeans. Jeans weren't for tonight. She went out and sat on the balcony, letting the warm evening air drift over her tired body. The air smelt of oleander and jasmine and the salt of the sea. It soothed her tension, enabling her to wait with a measure of composure.

Then Leeton was with her, a Leeton she had seen in photographs but never for real, with his dark skin and harsh features accentuated by the starkness of evening wear. His eyes smiled at her, and their look told her she was beautiful. She? Ellie Michaels? She must be dream-

ing. She met his eyes again and knew it was true. To
him she was lovely.

There was no time for words. Behind Leeton came
their host and a dinner trolley. A white linen cloth was
thrown over the wooden outdoor table. Candles were
set in place and dinner was served.

For years after Ellie would remember every mouthful
of that meal. There were prawns in crusty shells of
paper-thin batter tasting of lemon, and prosciutto and
melon served with tiny olives tasting of the sun-
drenched groves of Italy. Then there were gleaming
silver garfish, lying in a fragrant creamy sauce that
whispered around her mouth of the flavours of the sea,
served with tiny golden potatoes and a salad of mango
and orange and fruit that she had never tasted but
vowed she would taste again.

Through all, the champagne bubbled and Leeton
watched her like a benevolent genie indulging his starving prodigy — and she told him so.

'Or a wealthy uncle giving boarding-school treats.'
She smiled shyly up at him, and the warmth in his eyes
intensified.

'I don't feel like an uncle,' he said softly.

Ellie's colour deepened and she bent again to her
meal.

The champagne was making her dizzy, she thought.
It must be the champagne; nothing else could make her
feel like this. Then she looked up at Leeton and knew
that the champagne had nothing to do with it.

They ate field-fresh strawberries and clotted cream,
served in twisted bowls of chocolate. Then there were
huge clusters of frosted grapes and platters of biscuits
and Camembert and Brie and cheeses she had never
tasted. Their host served coffee, and beamed, and
beamed again, and then they were left alone.

Silence. It went on forever. Dusk had deepened to

dark and a waning silver moon was rising to the east. Leeton sat back and watched the girl before him.

'Would you like a walk?' he said quietly. 'The sea is only a hundred yards down the track.'

Ellie looked shyly up at him. It was all she could do to make herself say the words. 'Yes, please.' It was a whisper.

It was enough. He stood and came around to draw her chair from the table.

They walked down the sandy track in silence. Leeton's hand held hers possessively. She was his, his hand told her. His hand claimed her.

They emerged from the overgrown garden track to a wide expanse of soft, warm sand. Beyond the sand were the rocks, then the sea.

'It's a sheltered lagoon,' Leeton told her, gesturing over the moonlit water. 'Tomorrow we'll swim.'

Ellie nodded mutely, her heart swelling in happiness. Tomorrow and tomorrow and tomorrow. . .

They wandered slowly down to the water's edge. Then Leeton turned her to face him. His hands held her at arm's length, his eyes searching hers.

'I need to apologise,' he told her. 'I've been every kind of damned fool. I love you, Ellie. I loved you from the moment I first laid eyes on you, and I wouldn't believe my heart.'

She placed a finger on his lips. 'I deserved your disbelief,' she told him. 'That article. . .and then Gordon. I had to deceive you. You understand that?'

'Now I do.' He sighed and his hands moved to span her waist. 'I should have seen it. All the signs were there.'

'You're a vet, Leeton,' Ellie told him lovingly, 'and you've never treated AIDS patients. I had, and for New York doctors AIDS is no longer an uncommon diagnosis.' She leaned against him, her breasts moulding to his chest. 'You couldn't have known. Poodles might get gastric ulcers, but as far as I know they don't get AIDS.'

'They don't,' he smiled. 'The only animal genetically close enough to humans to carry the virus is the chimpanzee, and chimpanzees don't get sick with it.'

Ellie sighed and nestled against the coarse fabric of his jacket. 'It's just as well,' she said softly. 'It occurred to me after Gordon's encounter with the leopard seal that he might have infected the seal population of the Antarctic. Too horrid to contemplate really. . .'

Leeton smiled and pulled her closer. 'Ellie, there's only one thing I don't understand. Why wouldn't you let me kiss you the day the ice-breaker came? If I remember correctly, you said you'd rather kiss a fish.'

She gave a rather undignified giggle and looked ruefully up at her love. She moved slightly so the moonlight shone on the fading scar on her arm.

'This happened the day Gordon was hurt,' she said simply. 'I was afraid I might be infected.'

His mouth twisted. 'And you wouldn't put me at risk.'

'I couldn't.' Her voice faded to a whisper and he bent his head to hear. 'How could I put you at risk? I loved. . . I love you.'

Silence. The waves ran softly up on to the sand, hissing and bubbling with the incoming tide. Leeton's smile had faded and his look was almost stern. 'Oh, Ellie.'

He bent and kissed the scar, then his hands tightened on her waist and he pulled her to him. Like a drowning man he searched for her and found her, his mouth devouring hers as if she was his last link to life, his last love.

She felt strength flow through him and desire and commitment. She opened her lips and welcomed his tongue, and her hands pulled him in to her, closer and closer. Joy was flowing from one to another, lighting the night, lighting their love. Then the seed of a thought flashed into her mind, and she pulled back, looking at him uncertainly in the moonlight.

'Leeton, don't you want to know that I've been tested for AIDS?' she asked uncertainly.

'I don't need to,' he told her.

'Wh—why not?' Her body was aching for him. She had discarded her flimsy sandals. The sand was soft on her feet and the swell of the ocean was singing in her ears.

He smiled as his hands tightened around her, pulling her in to him once more. 'For a start, you're not still saying you'd rather kiss a fish,' he admitted. He raised a hand and ran it across the soft skin of her cheek, down across her shoulder, then let it lie on the smooth swell of her breasts. Ellie could feel her breasts rise to his touch. He bent to kiss her lightly on the hair. 'And it can no longer matter. We're one, you and I. We've known it for two years, my beautiful Ellie, and we might as well admit it. Whether you have any other dark secrets lurking in your closet—it doesn't matter, because you're my love.'

His hands were pulling her body in to him, and Ellie felt herself floating on a pinnacle of joy. The world had stopped. There was only this moment—this man.

'As soon as we're back in New York we'll make it legal,' Leeton said thickly, and she could feel the ragged desire in his voice. The time for words was all but over. 'But you are my wife and I'm your husband as surely as any legal ceremony can make us. We're one, Ellie. You and me. Forever.'

Ellie's heart sang within her. She laid her hand on his cheek and ran her fingers over the stern contours.

'I have been tested,' the told him huskily. 'And I'm clear.'

'That's perfect,' he said, and he was kissing the deep hollow of her breasts. 'Because I'll admit I'd like children. Marbuck would like them too,' he added thoughtfully.

'Children?' Ellie choked on laughter. Her hands were holding him to her and her body was doing strange things. Somewhere a fire had been lit and it was growing . . .growing. . . 'How. . .how many?'

Leeton's fingers had found the zip of her dress and his mouth was deepening the kiss. 'A dozen or so?' His voice was husky. The soft folds of white fabric fell away and the moonlight fell on her naked breasts. The night belonged to them. There was the moon and the ocean, a man and a woman and nothing more.

'A dozen. . .' Ellie's voice was a breathless squeak and her body was alight to his touch. What was he doing? What was happening to her? Her legs were jelly and she was sinking, sinking to the soft, caressing sand. She gasped as the sand received her. She was fighting for her voice, fighing for control, then, suddenly not fighting at all. . .

'If you want them too,' he said softly. 'And if they're good travellers. . .'

'Good travellers?' Leeton's hands were holding her body to him. She was moulding to him, melting under his touch.

'We have places to go,' he said huskily, his mouth in her hair. 'Think of the work we can do together, Ellie. A medical team.'

'You mean. . .' She pulled away from him, her eyes searching in the moonlight. Suddenly what he was saying was desperately important. She had been down this road with Sam. 'You mean you want me to keep being a doctor?'

'You are a doctor, Ellie,' he told her. 'And I love you. Therefore I love you being a doctor. . .'

'But my work might stop me doing the things you want.'

'Your work is as important as my work.' He was

stroking her hair, his fingers intertwining in the soft strands. He moved to kiss again the gentle swell of her naked breasts, his tongue teasing each nipple in turn. 'I think we should work out what we want to do, Ellie,' he whispered. 'Together.'

'Oh, Lee. . .'

'Oh, Ellie. . .' his voice mocked lovingly. And Ellie was lost.

'Leeton?' Her voice came in a ragged gasp.

'Yes, my love?' His lips were moving down. . . down. . . Ellie gave a sob of pure pleasure.

'I think I've worked it out.'

'What?'

'What I want,' she managed.

'What we want?' he teased her.

Her hands reached frantically to pull him to her. Her body arched to him. She moulded to him as if they were meant for each other—a man and a woman created as one.

Then whatever control she had was gone. She had no further use for it. The rhythm of the sea became her rhythm and the stars and the moon were part of her.

'What do we want, then, Ellie?' Leeton's voice was a groan of ecstasy.

She didn't answer. Even if she could, there was no need.

4 MEDICAL ROMANCES AND 2 FREE GIFTS

FROM MILLS & BOON

Capture all the drama and emotion of a hectic medical world when you accept 4 Medical Romances PLUS a cuddly teddy bear and a mystery gift - absolutely FREE and without obligation. And, if you choose, go on to enjoy 4 exciting Medical Romances every month for only £1.70 each! Be sure to return the coupon below today to: **Mills & Boon Reader Service, FREEPOST, PO Box 236, Croydon, Surrey CR9 9EL.**

✄ — — — — — — [**NO STAMP REQUIRED**] — — — — — —

YES! Please rush me 4 FREE Medical Romances and 2 FREE gifts! Please also reserve me a Reader Service subscription, which means I can look forward to receiving 4 brand new Medical Romances for only £6.80 every month, postage and packing FREE. If I choose not to subscribe, I shall write to you within 10 days and still keep my FREE books and gifts. I may cancel or suspend my subscription at any time. I am over 18 years.
Please write in BLOCK CAPITALS.

Ms/Mrs/Miss/Mr _____ **EP53D**

Address _____

_____

Postcode _____ Signature _____

mps
MAILING
PREFERENCE
SERVICE

MEDICAL ROMANCE

The books for enjoyment this month are:

A BORDER PRACTICE Drusilla Douglas
A SONG FOR DR ROSE Margaret Holt
THE LAST EDEN Marion Lennox
HANDFUL OF DREAMS Margaret O'Neill

♥ ♥ ♥ ♥ ♥

Treats in store!

Watch next month for the following absorbing stories:

JUST WHAT THE DOCTOR ORDERED Caroline Anderson
LABOUR OF LOVE Janet Ferguson
THE FAITHFUL TYPE Elizabeth Harrison
A CERTAIN HUNGER Stella Whitelaw